SECURING HIS STAR

LEATHER PERSUASION SERIES 10

BY

REXI LAKE

D1519763

DEDICATION

Still -

For all those whose way of loving is unconventional.

Love is individual. Love is unconditional.

Love is unconventional.

Also -

Fall in love often and hard.

Love how you choose.

Love who you choose.

Love all you choose.

Love with all you are.

If you love and are loved in return, you are one of the lucky ones.

SECURING HIS STAR

CHAPTER ONE

~DANICA~

"Welcome to the Leather Persuasions Resort!" The flamboyant flourish and bow that accompanied the greeting was everything I expected from the man I'd spent many a phone call getting to know well. "My dear, Danica," Lance greeted as he stepped forward to assist me off the boat and onto the dock that served as the entrance to the exclusive resort.

I took his hand and smiled in greeting as I took my first step onto the property of the place I'd spent years wondering about. "Lance," I said warmly. "It's so wonderful to finally see you."

The tall man leaned forward and kissed my cheek. "My dear, it is *so* wonderful to be *seen*! My, but we have so much to talk about, I'm sure. But the gossip will simply have to wait until we get you settled." He tucked my arm around his and after giving swift directions to the porters lurking nearby for my luggage, he led me to the shore.

"Oh, yes. I'm sure we have much to talk about," I agreed. After all, Lance was *the* person to know at the resort. While the man didn't divulge much about himself personally, he knew everything and everyone to do with the place that he ran with pristine and exacting instructions.

"Come, let's give you a quick tour while I tell you about the plans I've put in place," he told me. His accent, that European flair, was false, I knew. But it fit him so very well.

"Plans? Lance, I only asked for you to secure an introduction anonymously," I chided.

"Psh! My sweet woman, you *know* I simply cannot arrange anything so simple as that. Besides, if you wish to capture his attention, then you must be very specifically placed." Lance patted my hand and directed their walk, pointing out the spots that I would need to know about along the way. "Over there are some outdoor play areas that can be secluded if you alert someone ahead of time by reserving a space. While many of our outdoor accommodations are first come, first serve - or rather, serviced - we do offer some areas that can be created to your specifications." He sent me a wink as he grinned at his own play on words.

I looked toward the small groves and the sandy beach that extended beyond those strategically placed trees. I could hear a few guests taking advantage of the side of the resort that allowed full nudity and adult entertainment. "And the cottages on this side?" I asked.

"These are the higher end ones. Your man usually reserves one of these so he can play without interruptions. Though he has also booked the occasional dungeon room too. That's rare. Although, I'm sure you've done your research on those options, haven't you?" Lance sent a coy smile in my direction as he spoke.

"Now, Lance, you know a lady doesn't kiss and tell," I answered with a laugh.

He chuckled. "Oh, Dani, but that's just not fair!"

"You'll survive without the juicier details," I assured him.

He put a hand over his heart and looked at me, crestfallen. "But it's the *juiciest* details that keep me in the best spirits."

I laughed, as he intended me to do. "Lance, my sweet, matchmaking friend, I know you have plenty of people to feed you all the gossip that you need to stay on top of things."

"Oh, well," he paused and considered my words. "I suppose that is true," he conceded. "But, I hope I at least get an invitation to the wedding when it happens. I do love getting fancied up!"

"I think you're getting very ahead of yourself. We don't even know if he'll be interested."

"Don't we?" he asked, that secretive and knowing smile on his face.

"Lance, what do you have planned?" I asked, my eyes narrowing.

"Nothing extravagant, I assure you."

"Everything you do is extravagant, Lance."

"Certainly not! Some things are quite mundane."

I eyed my companion with suspicion. I knew getting Lance involved in the plan would lead to more than I thought was necessary, but now I was wondering exactly what it was that the man had up his sleeve.

"Don't worry so much, Dani," Lance assured. "Everything will work out as it should."

"You sound very certain of that."

"My dear, when you have done my type of work for the number of years I have done it - which I will not be divulging - then there is a ninety-nine point nine percent chance of the intended outcome occurring with great success. And I am highly successful."

It wasn't a boast. I knew Lance was one of the most sought after matchmakers for the kink community. He could find a person exactly what they needed, even if they didn't know they needed it.

"Okay. I'll trust you to at least provide a suitable introduction. But I know this man and even your skills might not be enough to get him to extend the two vacations of his to something more permanent."

Lance sighed. "That part, my dear Dani, will depend on how open you are with him. If you put all of yourself into this, you'll reap the rewards you so justly deserve."

I bit my lip and kept quiet as he finished the little tour, ending at a small cottage on the other side of the resort. I'd considered booking one of the hotel rooms, but I enjoyed my own privacy a little too much to share a wall or two with anyone, even if they were enforced and soundproof.

My luggage was already inside by the time we arrived and Lance assured me that the small kitchenette was stocked with enough items to last the rest of the day at the least.

"Rest up. Tomorrow the fun begins!" He clapped his hands with excitement, making me eye him quizzically. "Oh, don't be a spoilsport, Dani. You will be enjoying everything your heart desires sooner than you think." He pressed a kiss to my cheek and waved his fingers. "I will see you in the morning for breakfast and tell you all about your plans then," he promised.

I nodded. "Have a good evening, Lance," I told him.

Shutting the door behind him as he left to return to his resort duties, I leaned back against the sturdy wood and looked at the comfortable space before me. The cottage was exactly what I expected - quaint and comfortable. The small sitting area had a cozy couch perfect for curling up on. The small kitchen was fully equipped and stocked as well. And the bedroom, I sighed when I caught that first glimpse of the king-sized bed draped with decorative netting for a romantic ambience. I knew Lance had set this up for me. The man was king at understanding the people he provided for.

Turning, I grabbed the suitcase I'd dragged back to the room with me and opened it up to unpack. I pulled out the softest clothes I owned and carefully placed the items in the drawers of the dresser. I anticipated I'd need them, but even if I didn't for the reasons I hoped, they were the most comfortable to lounge in. After unpacking, I wandered back to the living space and took my small carry on to the little table. I'd taken a short vacation from the firm, but I still had to watch my emails. Clients' needs didn't pause just because I was out of town. My handful of active cases still needed attention. And the ones that were not active could become active at any moment. As a lower level associate, I didn't have quite the same luxury of others doing my work for me, but I also didn't have the caseload that came from being higher up either. Mixed blessings, I supposed.

Opening my email showed that nothing had gone sideways during my travel from Miami to the island of St. John. That was a blessing. When you worked in a litigation practice, things didn't always go smoothly. I'd learned that very quickly when I'd been *his* personal assistant.

Patrick O'Shaughnessy. *The* defense attorney for the greater Miami area, and quite frankly, Florida in general. His was the name on the letterhead and his was the firm to be a part of if you wanted to get anywhere. When I'd first applied to the only opening there was, I'd had no idea what I was getting into. I knew I wanted my foot in the door though. I'd just finished my first year of college and I was determined to become a lawyer that people wanted to represent them. The O'Shaughnessy firm was part of that plan. And it had been a stroke of luck that I'd found the opening for an assistant. And then I'd met *him*.

He was thirty to my green nineteen at the time. I knew I was infatuated. But I didn't care. I wanted him to notice me. I learned quickly that the thing he noticed was hard work. Lucky for me, I excelled at being not just good at my job, but the best. I learned his habits and needs and anticipated them before he could ask. It took a year, but the more I excelled, the more he started to pause before and after barking his orders. And then that day I'd been wanting had finally happened; I don't think I'll ever forget the way he stopped in front of me and spoke to me. It wasn't to bark orders or make demands for himself or the firm. And it wasn't even a conversation. It was simple and direct, like he was. A compliment.

"Good job, Danica. That tip about the money being moved helped our case."

Then he'd walked away. Back into his office, leaving me slack-jawed and staring after him. I'd sat down in my chair rather abruptly as my knees went a little weak in the hope that maybe he would finally start noticing me as more than a simple assistant.

He had. After that he had started to include me in some of his meetings to take notes and observe. It was slow, but it was something. But it wasn't exactly what I wanted either. Sure, I still had my goals of being a lawyer and seeing my name on letterhead someday. But I wanted him too. At least, that was what I thought in my girlish fantasies of being swept off my feet by my boss.

But my fairytale fantasies quickly ended after my curiosity got the better of me. I'd booked his resort vacation twice a year for five years before I ever discovered what I was booking. I hadn't even known the real name of the place. The phone number Patrick had given me the first time was obviously a special number. The voice on the other end only answered with the initials of the place, not the name. I'd looked up "LP Resort" online a few times and had been inundated with the number of places that had those initials.

One night, a few months after I'd switched positions and a new woman took the personal assistant job, I'd gone to happy hour with a handful of colleagues. The conversation had turned to the boss, as it often did when there were a bunch of tipsy women getting together from the office. Most were paralegals and

SECURING HIS STAR

assistants, but there were also two other lawyers this time too. When Nikki, the new assistant, brought up the mysterious vacation she'd just booked for Patrick, all eyes had swung my way.

"Sorry," I'd told them. "I know nothing more than she does."

"But you were his assistant for years! How can you not know?" Mindy had asked. She was one of the assistants for the family too. Her boss was Patrick's uncle, Jameson O'Shaughnessy. He handled a number of his own big name clients, but sometimes he and Patrick collaborated.

"I know what I was," I'd remarked wryly.

"I bet it's not a well-known place. It's probably so exclusive that you can't even go without being recommended or something," Nikki had mused. "He doesn't date. Maybe he's gay and he meets his lover there or something."

I and all the other women had laughed at that. No way in hell was Patrick O'Shaughnessy gay. He oozed sex appeal, at least to me, but more than that, if he had a secret sex life, his grandmother would be the first to know about it. That woman was as tough as nails and as smart as any of the lawyers she'd married and raised. Rumor had it that the woman was the reason O'Shaughnessy's was as big a name as it was. She'd married the first O'Shaughnessy lawyer not long after he'd started a fledgling practice in the streets of Miami. She wasn't Irish, like he was, she was half Cuban and had a flair that had attracted the man into getting down on one knee. Then she'd brought him her family's business - Cuban cigars weren't legal, but her family had learned how to make the best cigars in America that were comparable to the ones no longer crossing from the island.

Now, the woman was still a force to be reckoned with and she had a standing lunch date with each of her children and grandchildren in the firm. And they were all there in some capacity. Patrick, the eldest son of Jackson O'Shaughnessy, had taken the reins of the business from his father when he'd retired early. No one knew exactly why he'd retired so young, although there were plenty of rumors.

The conversation had dipped away, but I couldn't help but think more about it later. When I'd gone home that night, still just tipsy enough to be without my best judgment, I'd called the number that was still programmed in my phone.

"LP Resort, this is Lance, how may I help you?"

I almost lost my courage and hung up, but something stopped me. And instead of hanging up, I asked the question I'd been thinking for far too long. "I was wondering if you could give me some more information about your resort," I said.

"This line is typically called only by those who are supposed to stay oblivious to their boss's plans. Why should I break my policy and provide you with any more information?"

SECURING HIS STAR

"Perhaps, because I'm not calling for my boss. In fact, the man I used to schedule this for is no longer my direct boss and I don't handle the scheduling anymore. If your policy is intended to protect the specific plans of my boss, who is no longer my boss, then that nullifies the policy. Doesn't it?" Okay, I'd definitely been more than a little tipsy because the logic of my argument was half false. Patrick was still my boss, after all, just not in the same way.

But somehow it had worked. And suddenly, my girlish fantasies had taken a much darker turn. The LP Resort wasn't a beach vacation or a spa to relax at. It was a highly exclusive kink resort that catered to all manner of fetishes and allowed people to explore their darkest, deepest, kinkiest desires in a safe and totally private environment. And I was more than intrigued. Maybe the alcohol played a small part in that initial interest, but it had only opened the door for me.

Lance became my guide into the kink world, even setting me up with a membership at a local dungeon where I could meet others and learn about the lifestyle. And for over a year I dove headfirst into the experiences of it all. A full year of attending munches, dungeon events, and classes about things like bondage, impact play, choosing partners, and anything and everything a person could think of. I'd immersed myself in it until I'd found the things that not only appealed to me, but lit me up from the inside.

I found play partners and had some enjoyable encounters. But nothing ever clicked for more. And strangely, I realized that I'd never once seen Patrick at an event.

One evening, during one of the now routine calls with Lance, I'd taken the next plunge and asked about my boss. Lance had jumped at the curiosity in my voice and suddenly all my secret desires were spilling out.

Two months later, I found myself sitting at a table in a cozy cottage on the property of the LP Resort. One more day. My heart was racing at the thoughts that filled my mind. The dreams and wants that circled through me until I wasn't sure what I wanted more or first. Or even what to expect from him.

I signed off my email, closing the laptop and going to the kitchen to find myself a drink. Taking a bottle of water from the fridge, I went out onto the small deck and looked toward the sound of the ocean. Not far beyond my little bit of privacy was the beach and the warm waves of Trunk Bay. And somewhere, just crossing the water perhaps, was Patrick. On his way to the resort for one of his vacations. Lance had said that each time Patrick gave him a few weeks' notice and requested a meeting with two or three submissive women that matched his needs. From there, he chose someone to spend his ten days with.

A shiver trailed down my spine. I didn't know all of his desires, but Lance had said many of my kinks lined up with his. I

SECURING HIS STAR

wondered which ones those were. Would he enjoy bondage? Or perhaps he was partial to the primal play that often left marks. I would find out soon; I only hoped when he learned my identity, it didn't cost me my job and the man I wanted. Ten days was all I would get unless I could convince him that the kinks he enjoyed didn't have to stay on the island.

CHAPTER TWO

~PATRICK~

In the small seaplane, I let myself shed the persona I wore everyday. The next ten days were my time to be the truest version of myself. Ruthless and aggressive in the courtroom, there was a side of me that I contained except for the days I allowed myself the luxury of stepping away from the rest of the world and embracing the sadistic side that enjoyed bringing a woman to her knees, filling her eyes with tears, and covering her body with endless marks.

The seaplane started the short descent to the waters below and I pulled the simple black mask I used into place. My face wasn't as famous as a movie star's or a rock star's, but I was known enough in my world that keeping my identity secret was a necessity. I required the same of any submissive that I interviewed or played with as well. My time spent at the Leather Persuasions Resort was kept completely separated from my everyday life. Nothing crossed that line. I made sure of it.

I felt the skis under the plane hit the water. The slight bounce as it settled on the waves was a welcome feeling. The last vestiges of my civility were left in the air behind me. The plane pulled up to the dock and I stood. My bags would be sent to the cottage I used each time I visited, but I had plans before I made my way there. Stepping onto the path that would take me to the hotel, I left Patrick O'Shaughnessy on the plane and assumed the anonymous mantle that let me feed the needs I kept concealed the rest of the year.

"Ah, Sir S." Lance greeted me as I walked through the doors.

"Lance," I returned, nodding at him. "I trust you have my private room ready for my needs?" I always made the most of my time by initiating an agreement as soon as I arrived. It allowed for more time to be spent in the pleasurable pursuits of pain and release.

"Don't I always?" He asked, looking affronted.

"You do, Lance." There was something slightly off about the other man's expression though. I couldn't quite put my finger on it, but something had me looking at him more closely.

"Of course I do," he said, waving his hand at a nearby service sub. The resort staffed plenty of submissive workers. I had done my research on the place when I was looking for my escapes. The LP was top in services provided, and that included the people as well as the spaces for play. "Michelle will take you back and get you anything you need. There are two applicants that match your qualifications this time. I'll send in the first one in ten minutes."

"Very good," I said, nodding in approval. Only two was unusual as there were typically three or four to interview, but since I trusted Lance to provide women that suited my specific needs, I knew no one else had met the rigid requirements the man set up.

The tall submissive woman that I followed led me to a room situated behind the main dining room of the hotel. Like all the other rooms, the walls were reinforced with soundproofing materials to ensure privacy for those inside. "Bring a pitcher of water and three glasses, then you may go," I told her. I preferred to conduct my interviews in total privacy. It kept even less people aware of my preferences.

I didn't bother to pay attention to the woman as she left. Instead, I took my time to look at the few instruments that had been laid out to my specifications. Picking up one of the wooden paddles, I tested the weight in my hand. It was heavy, but not too heavy. It would provide a solid *whap* against a good ass. But what brought a smile to my face was the combination of holes in the wood and studs that stuck out just enough to bruise flesh and provide a sting as well as the thud.

I set the paddle down and picked up the flogger that lay beside it. My hand curled around the leather wrapped handle. Solid and thick strips of leather hung from the other end with more studs along each strip. Interspersed with the leather straps were a half dozen chains, their links solid loops of metal that wouldn't break the skin, but would leave some thick welts and bruises behind. I felt my lips curl into a smile. Oh yes, this one would do well for my interviews.

The water was delivered and the woman who had led me to the room disappeared as ordered. I poured a glass for myself and took a long sip of the cool liquid. The anticipation curled inside me as I waited. It was always like that. Each interview was a thirty minute review and test. Since the specifications I required were rigid, I didn't need to go through the list of likes and limits. Those were reviewed with the women by Lance before they got to me. The majority of my interview was testing a woman's pain threshold. If she cried, called a safeword, or passed out, she was not the right one for me to play with.

The doors opened and the first woman walked in. There was a nervous bounce to her step and a shifting of her eyes that almost made me sigh. Either she was much better on paper, or Lance's skills were slipping. Bright blonde curls floated around her shoulders as she approached; she was perhaps five-three or so, and slim. Too slim for my tastes. I would have to be careful with someone like her. The smaller frame might not withstand my preferences.

"Can you handle a beating?" I asked, without any sort of preamble or platitudes.

"S-sir?" she stuttered in surprise.

I stood and approached her. Walking in a circle around her like a predator eyeing my prey. "Can you handle a beating?" I asked again, my voice dipping lower. I did not enjoy asking a question twice. Not at home and certainly not with a sub that should have already known that information.

"Um, I think so." She barely whispered the words.

I sighed. "I don't," I told her. "You may go."

I shook my head as she all but ran from the room.

Maybe she wasn't meant to come into my interview. It was the only explanation as to her presence. She was definitely not on par with the others Lance had sent me in the past. Either she'd been the closest option or she was not one of mine.

I glanced at the watch on my wrist. Timing was everything. If she had been my first interview, then I had twenty-seven minutes before the next woman appeared. I sat back down on the couch and let myself relax into the cushions. Closing my eyes, I indulged the fantasy I had of owning a particular woman. Eleven years younger than me and eager to please. It was that eagerness that made me hard. The intelligence she had didn't diminish with her service. It enhanced it. She'd found ways to provide things I didn't realize I needed. But that was work. And I never mixed work and pleasure.

Even before I'd separated it so thoroughly. Danica Stern made me want to cross that line.

Those expressive brown eyes of hers and that dark hair that I wanted to grip tight in my fist haunted my dreams. And those pouty, fuck me lips that were always tipped just slightly into a secretive little smile. I wanted to taste them. But it was her body that brought me to the edge. Curves and thick. If she could handle pain, her body could take it. I would bet money on that. But not everyone liked pain the way I liked to give it. I was a sadist. I liked to see bruises and welts form on pretty, unmarked flesh. I liked to watch the skin turn fiery red and feel it burn beneath my palm. It was my high. And breaking a woman open with that pain and seeing her find her release from it was a beautiful thing. It fed me like nothing else could.

I closed my eyes and thought back to that first day. The hiring of my assistant had been left to HR. I'd been too busy without an assistant to find the time to do interviews myself. When I'd walked into the office and found her sitting at the desk outside my personal office, I'd almost paused my steps. Almost. But I had better control than that. And even if she made me want to loosen the reins of that control, I couldn't afford to do that. So, instead, I'd wrapped myself in steel - metaphorically, of course - and refused to consider the thoughts except in the darkest recesses of my mind and the occasional fantasy I allowed out when I went to the island.

The fantasy that had her strapped to a cross, her back covered in my marks. Her body, mine to hurt and mine to pleasure. Her tears soaking the ground as her body grew wet with need and smeared her thighs. I could see it in my mind so clearly. It made me so fucking hard thinking about it. It drove me. Even if I didn't see her daily the same way I had for years, she had left an imprint on everything in my space. There was nowhere I could look without seeing her. The desks. The chairs. The filing cabinets. The organization of my office was nowhere near the level it had been during her tenure as my assistant. But somehow, everything seemed to hold her scent. It took everything in me to not have her added to my cases as an associate to do the lower level research. Everyone expected it; in fact, Danica had been the one to tell me *not* to do it.

"I mean it, Patrick. I'm taking the associate position because I want to work here. But moving forward, I don't want any help. Being your assistant means everyone is going to expect that I get special treatment. I don't want my colleagues looking at me like I didn't earn my place."

She'd even stressed her words with pointed fingers in my direction. I'd agreed, but quite honestly, I wondered how anyone could think she hadn't earned her place. The woman had managed to finish her undergrad work, law school, and pass the bar in less than six years. She was the hardest worker I'd ever seen and intelligent beyond most of the attorneys we hired. If she'd allowed me to give her the cases to work on, she would be halfway to becoming a partner already. Hell, I wouldn't have blinked if the rest of the family had said she could tack her name onto the letterhead. She was just that damn good. Plus my grandmother loved her. When Abuela took a liking to someone, that person inevitably became a part of the family anyway. Danica could have taken the easy way up the ladder. Her stubborn sass kept her on the bottom instead. Damn woman. Damn fine, sassy, smart woman.

A knock on the door pulled me from my thoughts. "Enter," I called out. Had it been long enough for the second interviewee to show up?

The door opened and I almost lost my breath. The woman that stepped into the space wore the requisite mask, concealing enough of her features to distort any possible recognition. But I had spent seven years looking at much more than the woman's face. I'd memorized her body, the way she moved, the way she spoke. Her eyes blinked up at me with a knowledgeable innocence that I had seen before, but never in the context I had now.

"Hello, Sir. My name is Star."

Star. Irony almost made me chuckle. She was that. And either she was completely oblivious to my identity or she knew. Either way, it was Lance who absolutely was playing a dangerous game. I stood, my heart beat slowing as I found the control I needed for what came next. Walking toward her, I watched as her eyes lowered first, away from mine. Then her head dipped down. Her hands were clasped in front of her. From a distance, she would appear calm, serene even. But closer inspection made it clear she was nervous. Her fingers were tightly gripped together, the knuckles white with tension.

"Do you enjoy pain, Star?" I asked her, walking around her. I took my time, admiring the body I'd long fantasized about. Now, I was seeing it more than ever before. The short skirt barely covered her ample ass. And the strappy bikini top would easily fall away if I pulled on the right string.

"Yes, Sir," she answered. Her tone was soft, but it was confident.

"How much?" I asked. I flexed my fingers, itching to reach out and touch what I'd never allowed myself to consider touching before.

"Quite a lot, Sir," she answered. Her head remained bowed, her eyes steadfastly locked on a spot on the floor in front of her.

"What instruments?" I asked. If she knew, she was doing a damn fine job of appearing oblivious.

"Barehanded, paddles, floggers, canes, a crop once."

I was surprised. I had anticipated a lesser degree of knowledge. Of course, I hadn't anticipated even a kernel of knowledge of this kind of thing in *her* head. To hear that she not only knew about such things but had experienced them first hand made me wonder.

"Which do you prefer?" I asked. I moved back in front of her. Clasping my hands behind my back, I waited for her answer.

"My preference depends on my need, Sir." Her eyes were still cast downward, subservient. "Sharper pain or stinging is my favorite. Sometimes the wider, more thuddy impact is better to bring me higher over a longer period of time. But it does take much longer."

Her answer was comprehensive. I appreciated that. Now I needed to see just how much was true or not. "Lance explained the process to you, I assume?" I asked.

She nodded. "He said you would require a demonstration."

"That's correct. Is there anything you wish to know before that?"

She bit her lip and I braced myself for the possibility she would back out. She raised her head slightly and met my gaze from beneath those thick dark lashes of hers. "Do you draw blood?" she asked.

I raised a brow. Not what I was expecting. "I do not use instruments that have excessively sharp edges. No knives, razors, or anything like that. I have some instruments for impact play that can split the skin if used improperly or wrongly placed. Blood is not my first preference; but is sometimes present. Is that a limit?"

She shook her head. "Not the blood. But sharp instruments like knives and needles are. I am not partial to the slice of blades or the pricks of needles or tacks. I don't mind if my skin breaks from the lash of a whip or cane. And I do enjoy the dulled studs that can be pointed without being sharp."

I nodded. Knives, needles, and the like were not in my preference either, so it wouldn't be a problem for me. Although I knew it was possible to handle play like that without damaging the submissive, I also knew quite well how knives and sharp instruments could leave lasting and deadly results as well. "The table next to the wall has four items on it. Choose one and separate it from the others. Then kneel on the bench and raise your skirt."

She nodded in response. "Yes, Sir." I watched her walk to the table and waited until she'd followed through on my orders before I approached. I averted my eyes from the flesh she revealed as she hiked up her skirt. If I looked before I had the instrument in my hands, I would forget my purpose. *Fuck,* I thought to myself. Fucking her was exactly what I wanted to do. But that was playing with fire. I wasn't afraid of the flames, but getting burned could lead to some unhappy consequences at home.

She'd chosen the paddle. It was a good choice, though not as stingy as she had said she preferred. Perhaps the choice was her test as well.

"I'll start with ten strikes," I told her, coming up beside her. I put my free hand on the small of her back. "Grip the bars to steady yourself. I want you to count each stroke. When I'm done with the ten, you can say 'Thank you, Sir' or 'More please, Sir.' Do you understand?"

"Yes, Sir," she answered.

I waited until her fingers were securely wrapped around the provided bars. Then I settled the paddle in my hand and swung.

The *thwap* of wood against flesh was loud in the silent room.

"One," she said.

I swung again, adding a little more strength behind it.

Thwap.

"Two."

Thwap. Thwap.

"Three. Four."

I frowned. Her voice sounded even, strong. She wasn't falling into a headspace. I added more strength, this time taking pleasure in the way her skin was warming beneath the impact. Her flesh was a slight pink at the impact zone. I'd allowed the paddle to strike fully, widening the area of impact and spreading the burn. I'd also used the non-studded side.

Thwap.

"Five."

I flipped the paddle around and shifted my body. The next stroke landed on her right cheek alone. This time, the studs added to the impact.

Thwap.

"Six."

Thwap. Thwap. Thwap. Thwap.

Left. Right. Left. Right.

"Seven. Eight. Nine. Ten."

Her ass was just starting to turn rosy, but her voice, though it held a little more contentment, was still strong.

"What do you say, Star?" I asked, though I was certain of her answer.

"More please, Sir," she answered readily.

I rubbed my hand along her spine. "Ten on each side," I told her. "Count from eleven."

"Yes, Sir."

Beneath my hand she was still relaxed and calm. No tension in her muscles or her limbs that I could see or feel. She didn't anticipate the pain. That was a good thing. Tension of her muscles could cause injury instead of pleasure.

This time I let myself enjoy the delivery more. I stayed watchful and careful of her responses, but increased the strength and speed of the strokes. After the first ten on the right side, the skin was red and a few spots in the area told me some blood vessels had popped. The second set of ten on the left did the same. And finally, about halfway through that, her body changed. Just slightly. But enough to tell me that she did in fact enjoy pain. More than enjoy it, she could take it. Instead of being relaxed, she'd become pliant. I knew if I continued, she would begin to shift into eager, leaning into the impact instead of just taking it.

I smoothed my hand over her ass after the second set. Feeling the heated flesh and hearing her sigh at the contact.

"What do you say?" I asked.

"More please, Sir," she answered. Although she wasn't quite as steady as the first time, I could hear the need in her tone and the slight catch in her voice. She wasn't begging for it, but she wanted it. That hint of softness behind the request made me smile.

"Do you want to continue with the paddle?" I asked.

"If you wish, Sir." A non-response, but also a compliant one. And it told me that although she'd chosen the paddle, none of the other instruments were a limit for her. Including the flogger.

"Ten more. Then we will be done," I told her.

I would have changed to another instrument, but I didn't need to see any more. The interview was over for me. The woman I'd wanted to strap in place and mark up was not only offering herself up, she wanted what I could deliver. The question remained if she knew it was me. The next ten days would give me plenty of time to break her open and learn her secrets. Secrets I now needed to know.

"Yes, Sir," she answered.

I took my time with the final strokes. Letting the anticipation build up before delivering each one.

She counted them all. Though she slid a little more into a different headspace, it wasn't by much. Her voice was still stronger and more confident than I wanted her to be. I would enjoy finding the threshold that sent her tumbling away from coherence.

"What do you say?" I asked after the last stroke connected.

"Thank you, Sir," she answered. She looked up at me as she spoke. A smile played around the corners of her lips and made me consider rubbing my thumb over that pouty bottom one. But not yet. If she agreed, that would be something to explore with her later.

I rubbed my hand over her ass, turning my eyes to the red globes and enjoying the marks left behind. They were minimal, though she would feel sore for a few hours at least. Afterwards, I pulled her skirt back into place and helped her to stand.

She smoothed the front of her outfit and then waited. Calm. Submissive.

I put the paddle back on the table. The instruments would be delivered to my cottage once I left the room. Cleaned and ready for my use when I next desired it. I went to the water pitcher and poured a new glass, returning to her and offering the beverage.

"Do you have a room in the hotel?" I asked mildly.

"No, Sir. I have a cottage near the beach." She took a careful sip of the water after she spoke.

"If you agree to enter into this temporary service, will you also accept moving out of your cottage and into mine?" I stood before her and crossed my arms, considering.

"That won't be a problem, Sir," she answered.

"You understand that you would have to wear the mask at all times except in your room? That I require complete anonymity from an arrangement?"

"Yes, Sir." She kept her gaze averted from mine by sipping the water again. Was she that thirsty? Or did she know?

I nodded. "Very well. You can return to your cottage. Lance will be by to give you further information if I choose you. You'll know by this evening so if you wish to pursue another potential partner, you will have the opportunity to do so."

"Thank you, Sir," she said.

I watched as she left. That sweet ass of hers swaying with each step. She stopped at the table and placed her glass in the same place I had picked it up from. Then she was gone.

A few minutes after, Lance came in.

"Have you made a decision, Sir?" he asked.

I raised a brow in his direction. The unusual tone from earlier made sense now. "Lance," I chided.

"Sir?" he asked, playing innocent.

"You know. Does she?"

"I don't know which she you are referring to, Sir. Nor do I know what I'm supposed to know."

"Uh huh." So that's how he intended to play it. I could do that as well. For now. "Please deliver the usual instructions to Star. I expect her to be at my cottage for dinner. If she chooses to decline, I expect you will set up another set of interviews immediately."

No one had ever declined, but the order was standing in case it happened.

"Of course, Sir," Lance responded. "I'll get the paperwork together immediately."

I nodded and left as Lance gathered the water glasses and pitcher. I could hear him call out to one of the other employees to take care of my other items. But then I was out in the sunshine and walking toward my cottage. I had a few hours to relax and plan. Already my mind was spinning with ideas. I could feel my lips curving into a smile. It wasn't a nice one; it was dark, the kind of smile that Danica had often called sinister. She had no idea. But she would learn.

CHAPTER THREE

~DANICA~

Oh holy angels in heaven and hell, I thought to myself as I closed the door to my cottage behind me. I sunk to the floor, leaning against the cool wood. I didn't know how I'd managed to make it all the way back. My legs were weak from that interview. I hadn't been that nervous before, during, or after the job interview. But this? It had been exhilarating and terrifying all at once. And so incredibly hot. I was feeling the need for release. It wasn't overwhelming, but it was there. Forty strokes of a paddle weren't nearly enough, but it was just enough to feel something. Some little change inside me. A shift. I craved more than what he'd provided. But the taste of what he could give me was enough to make my mouth water and my body respond.

I hoped he chose me. I prayed for it. Not just because he was the man I'd fallen for before knowing this side of him. But because this side of him, at least the bit I'd just experienced, spoke to the side of me that craved pain and submission in my personal life. I needed to eat something. I was running on endorphins and all the energy I'd expended being anxious was going to bite me if I didn't get something in my stomach soon.

I kicked off the strappy heels I'd worn for the interview and stood carefully. I was just finishing up my sandwich and the apple slices I'd put together when there was a knock on the door. I grabbed the mask in case I needed it and went to look through the peephole.

"Lance," I greeted, opening the door with a hopeful smile.

He grinned and held up a small stack of paperwork. "I told you there was nothing to worry about, my dear," he boasted. "You have secured your ten days. So, I suggest you take the next few hours and read through these incredibly detailed pages of his contract and make sure you do indeed know what you are getting into." He set the pages on the counter and then faced me again.

"I know, Lance. Thank you, my friend."

"Oh, Dani, you sweetheart. You two are perfect for each other. I can't believe he was so dense to not see it sooner," Lance's hands fluttered in annoyance as he rolled his eyes. "Really, dear, some men can be very obtuse. They miss what is *right in front of their noses.*" He winked and added, "And other parts of their anatomy."

I laughed. "You're still not getting details," I told him.

"Ah," he exclaimed and waved a hand. "So stingy. I still expect my invitation though." He wiggled his fingers as he returned to the door. "Until next I see you, my dear. Do read those papers."

"I'm a lawyer, Lance. I read everything, including the fine print, at least twice."

He blew me a kiss before closing the door and leaving me in solitude once more. I allowed myself a brief happy dance and squeal of excitement. I had gotten my wish. Now I just needed to see it through.

~*~*~*~*~*~*~*~

It was six o'clock exactly when I knocked on the door of the cottage on the other side of the resort. I could see just from the outside that it was much bigger than the one I had. My orders had been clear on the papers I'd signed. I would present myself at six; my bags would be packed and someone would bring them to me later. The signed paperwork, which had been exceedingly thorough for a few days of play, had been delivered in advance of my arrival. That had been a requirement too.

Standing outside the door, uncertainty and anticipation warred inside me. I wasn't sure I was doing the right thing, but at the same time, I wanted this more than anything else. That was the plan, after all. Getting myself past the interview had been, I thought, the hardest part and the one I couldn't predict. But now

SECURING HIS STAR

that I had, I was nervous all over again. Nervous and needy. I wanted this man. I wanted him for who I knew he was, who I thought he was, and who I expected him to be. And that was before I knew his secret. Now, I wanted him for a whole list of additional reasons that had nothing to do with girlhood fantasies of princes and white horses.

The door opened and my mouth went dry. He'd gotten rid of the casual polo and slacks that he'd worn earlier. In its place was a pair of dark wash jeans that molded to his body like a second skin and nothing else. His chest was bare but for the dark hairs that made my palms itch to run my hands over. Would it be coarse, like the three-day stubble of a beard growing in. Or perhaps soft and fine, enticing me to stroke it endlessly. I raised my eyes carefully to his, trying to hide the desire that was swimming through me.

"You accepted," he stated. "Good. I expect you followed the other instructions as well."

It wasn't a question, but I answered him anyway. "Yes, Sir."

He stepped back and opened the door wider for me to enter. I tried to look around casually, but my heart was racing faster than a cheetah running across the sahara. The main room had a couch and that was the only thing it had that was similar to the cottage I'd been in. Aside from the couch, which was a dark leather piece, there were a number of pieces meant for anything but relaxation.

Chairs with straps on every side, benches in various inclines, a cross that leaned against the wall, and a sex swing hanging from the ceiling.

"I don't come here to relax, Star," he breathed in my ear. "I come here to let out the side of me that needs to bring pain and torture to someone."

I swallowed hard against the knot in my throat. The contract had said as much, but seeing the reality was more than a little overwhelming.

"I understand, Sir. I'm ready to begin when you wish." I heard my voice tremble just slightly as I spoke. That was not what I wanted, but perhaps he would understand as well.

"Are you hungry? Do you need to eat before we continue any play?" he asked.

I shook my head. "No, Sir. I had a late lunch. I will need to eat something afterwards though."

"Although you are here to endure what I wish to do to you, it would be remiss and negligent of me to not also ensure your well-being at the same time," he admonished. "If you begin to struggle and need anything, I expect you to use your safeword and alert me to that issue before it becomes a problem. Do you understand, Star?"

I nodded, my breath catching a little at the decidedly stern tone that sounded almost like a scolding. "Yes, Sir. I understand."

SECURING HIS STAR

"Good. To begin, I want to see exactly how much you can take," he said. I felt him move before he entered my vision. He strode ahead of me to the cross and the briefest of glances at me had me hurrying forward to him. "I want your clothing removed. You may fold it on the couch and then you will face the wall."

The impartial tone almost made me pause. But I caught myself. He didn't know who I was. He didn't know that my goal was more than a short experience with him. He didn't know any of that. *Yet.*

When my clothing was set aside, neatly folded, I stepped forward. I wasn't ashamed of my body, but there was definitely a vulnerability in shedding that last layer of protection and baring myself to his eyes that made me feel nervous. My fingers twisted together slightly as I approached the cross and the man. At first, I kept my eyes cast downward. But a glance up made me feel much better. His gaze was roaming over my body, not in judgment or boredom, but in interest and desire. He liked what he saw, he wanted what he saw. That knowledge flooded through me and I felt my confidence rise up.

"How would you like me, Sir?" I asked when I stood before him.

"Spread your legs as far as you can but keep your weight balanced on your feet," he instructed. There was a brief hitch in his tone; almost imperceptible.

"Yes, Sir," I murmured as I did as he said. When I was settled into a wider stance, he knelt down and methodically strapped first one ankle, then the other using soft straps with a belted cuff on the end to secure me.

I shivered a little as his hand caressed my ankle and calf. I knew it was a reflex, probably just him checking that my muscles weren't too taught and the straps secure but not tight. Still, that light stroking of his hand on me made me want to melt a little for him. A light touch would never be enough though.

He stood and his hands settled on my shoulders. "Stretch your arms to the sides and up," he instructed.

Now I could hear the control. He'd settled whatever it was that had caused that little hitch before. Now, the person in charge was very much in control. I lifted my arms into the position he dictated and waited silently as he finished securing me in place.

"Earlier, I allowed you to choose the instrument of your choice. The paddle, while nice for a good spanking, does not have the ability to inflict pain in quite the same manner as a cane or a flogger might. I won't jump straight to the cane for you, we will save that for another time. Tonight, I want to see how you take the flogger."

As he spoke, I could hear him moving about behind me. Then I heard the clink of metal and I knew he had the flogger that had been on the table at the interview. I must have shifted, perhaps tensed a little, because he chuckled.

"I won't be using this one tonight, Star. But it is one of my favorites. Tonight, I'll use the sister to this beauty. There are no chains; just thick leather. I had it made to my specifications. Forty of the ribbons are just that - ribbons of leather with knotted ends. But the rest of the tails are unique. Some are braided and thick. Some are knotted all the way down the length. And some have studs like the paddle you chose earlier. All of them are capable of providing you with the pain you are seeking."

He was right behind me again. I felt the handle of the flogger drag down my spine and a shiver followed, shaking me to the core and making everything inside me light up in anticipation.

"I don't want you to count. I don't want you to speak unless I ask a question. You have your safewords, should you need them. Otherwise, just feel. Close your eyes and relax. Let me see how far you go before you break open."

He moved the thick braid of my hair - the style was harsher than I preferred, but it kept the strands out of the way - to the side. Then he stepped back and I barely had a moment to think before the first blow struck my back and made me arch at the sudden sensations.

A gasp left my throat, but it was short and startled, not pained. Over and over again, he rained blows on me. Some hard, some soft, mixing it up until I couldn't predict what would come next. I couldn't fall into a rhythm either. I was fully aware and fully coherent. The burning on my back intensified as he continued, but I hadn't hit that level of pain that would send me spiraling yet either.

Ten minutes, twenty, an hour? I lost track of time as it seemed to both slow down and speed up until I could swear it had been both forever and a day or only a minute. He paused in his strikes. A very brief pause. And then, finally, pain sliced across my back with a strike that brought tears to my eyes. I gasped and choked on the unexpected inhale. Then he delivered a second blow that did the same. A third.

Each time, he paused just long enough for me to feel my muscles lose the tension of the last blow.

Five.

Ten.

I lost count, but the tears streaming down my cheeks brought ecstasy and relief. Pain blossomed and I wept as the leather and metal bit into my skin. I knew if I could see it, there would be welts - bright red and angry looking welts. Exactly what I wanted. Exactly what I needed. Even if he didn't know it was me he was striking, I could imagine he did. I could imagine that he knew he was giving me what I needed - *me. Danica.*

I felt him come closer. The air behind me shifted as the heat of him burned where my flesh was tender and sore.

One hand reached over my shoulder and cupped my chin, turning my face to the side. I lifted my tear-soaked lashes and found his dark green eyes boring into me with such intense focus that I nearly whispered his name. Instead, I bit my tongue and waited.

He stroked the handle of the flogger down my cheek, the rough movement making my breath catch and my heartbeat kick up again. I wanted to close my eyes and savor the feel, but I didn't dare look away. I couldn't.

"Can you take more?" he asked.

My skin vibrated as a shiver raced through me. The timber of his voice - a deep baritone with just a slight hint of that lilting Irish accent he had - was like fine whiskey to me. I could listen to him for hours, just drinking in the sounds of his words. But I didn't want words just then. I wanted more of the amazing pain he had given me.

"Yes, Sir. Please," I answered. My voice was hoarse from the tears. But there was no hesitation. He'd held back too much at first, but he'd held back nothing at the end. I hadn't fully broken yet though. I was still able to think. Able to feel. Able to reason. He hadn't taken me away yet. It took more than a few hard strikes of leather to do that. Much more. But he didn't know that yet. He didn't know that underneath the perfectly put together exterior was a woman that needed to feel pain with such intensity that it scared her.

He would find out. Or so I hoped.

He watched me for a long time. I could see him considering my response. Then he nodded and released me from his grip and his gaze. I felt the tension in the room mount as he stepped out of my sight. I did my best to stay still, quiet and waiting. The longer the silence lasted, the more I fought the desire to tense and look over my shoulder. Even if I did, there was a chance I wouldn't see him. And there was also the chance I would move at the wrong moment and the leather would hit where it shouldn't. I might not have been his, but I knew better. Even strapped as I was to the cross, unable to move more than the flexing of my joints and my head, I stayed still. And I waited.

And then, finally, I was rewarded. The silence of the leather moving through the air gave no warning. But the sudden flash of pain coupled with the slap of heavy straps against the back of my thighs had me gasping. He hadn't struck that spot before. The focus on my back had left me vulnerable. Now heat bloomed over the previously untouched skin. He rained ten strikes over the area in quick succession. Though he hadn't demanded it, I counted the lashes in my head. Each strike was heavier, harder. I felt my knees get weak as the muscles quivered where the leather struck. The

SECURING HIS STAR

knots at the end of each strap were designed for impact. But the strength he put behind each throw was taking the thud of thick leather to a place that was so much more painful. Impact and the edges of each leather strip struck with precision and force that left my skin striped, reddened, and burning. And it was bliss.

It was the burning that finally hit me hardest. He switched his focus back to my back, but the skin there had cooled just enough that the first hard strike made me cry out. After the third, it was a moan. The resurgence of heat on my overworked nerves pushed the burning of my flesh into a burning need for something entirely different.

I wanted fucked and filled with such intensity that for a few lashes, I lost my focus. The world blurred around me and the burning - inside and out - was all I could feel. My vision wavered, like the waves of heat over pavement on a hot Miami afternoon. Everything was shifting and I let my head drop forward to rest on the wall. It was my first concession. Until then, I hadn't leaned on anything. Even my weight had stayed balanced on my legs, spread though they were.

I thought I heard an inhale behind me when I did it. I could have imagined the noise, but the part of me that wanted him - all of him - grabbed at the possibility.

By the time he finished, I knew he had to be able to see how much it had taken to break me. He had to see how much I craved being beaten. My desire dripped down my legs. Though I hadn't begged, he'd brought me to the first ledge. To that space where pain took over and thinking became secondary to feeling.

I felt him come up behind me again. He didn't touch me this time though. His breath sounded in my ear as he leaned in. He was so close that I could have flexed my shoulders and his skin would touch mine.

"How long has it been since you've broken apart, Star?"

Star, that was the name Lance had given me for anonymity. He'd chuckled at the irony of it. I'd rolled my eyes then. But now? Now I wanted to hear Patrick say it again and again and again.

"It's been awhile, Sir," I answered honestly.

Six months to be exact. Six months of staying away from the clubs and dungeons. Of denying myself the pleasures of pain and release. Because I wanted to come to *him* without marks or bruises from anyone else. I wanted to be a blank canvas for him. And for me. Because if he didn't want me beyond the island, at least I would have the marks to remember our time together. Marks that wouldn't be made by anyone else. Marks that, at least for a little while, I could pretend meant I belonged to him.

CHAPTER FOUR

~PATRICK~

"**D**o you want to break for me?" I asked the question.

"Do you want to come apart?"

I heard her inhale as she struggled to breathe without begging. "Please, Sir. I would like that."

I flipped the flogger around in my hand and used the end of the shaft to trace across one of the longer raised red marks. Her cry was music in the thick silence around us. I repeated the movement, adding more pressure, and she shuddered as a whimper filled the room.

"If I touched your pussy right now, would I find you dripping with need, Star?" I asked harshly. "Would you be so wet that I could fuck you with the handle of this flogger and it would sink into you as easy as a knife through butter?"

She lifted her lashes and met my gaze. The brown orbs glistened with tears as they spilled down her cheeks. Her lips parted on a gasp as I pressed a knuckle against another mark. The skin wasn't broken, but she would wear the red lines across her flesh for a few days. I'd have to be more careful while those areas of her skin healed.

"If you want to come apart, you need to tell me how," I demanded.

"You," she gasped. "Please, Sir. I - Your fingers. Scratching." She leaned backwards, into the pressure I was already delivering.

It took me less than a moment to understand her request. I dropped the flogger and wrapped one arm around her hip and dipped my hand between her legs. I found her as wet and needy as I expected. I pushed two fingers into her grasping pussy and with my free hand, I drew my blunted nails and roughened fingers down her back. I dug deep into her flesh, leaving fresh marks behind, crossing over the harsher ones already there.

She cried out and her body jerked in the bonds that held her in place.

"Let go, Star," I demanded. I drew my fingers from her heat and slapped her back, just over one of those welts, as I pushed them deep again. I repeated that over and over as she shook against me, her high so close and just waiting for her to tumble over it. Each time I added to the slap. Gripping her skin, pinching it, scratching it. And then her cries and gasps jumped to another decibel and I felt her walls contract around my fingers so tightly I couldn't withdraw. "That's it," I murmured. I switched my harsher actions off and rubbed soothing circles over her reddened back. Her shaking slowed and her body shifted as she went languid against me.

I pulled my fingers from her greedy pussy and steadied her. "I need to release you from the cross, Star," I murmured. "Can you stand still for me for just a moment?"

She nodded, her head dropping forward and resting against the wall as she sagged forward a little.

I knelt and quickly released her ankles. Her wrists were next and I caught her as she stumbled backwards.

She hissed at the contact briefly, before she passed out in my grip. I grabbed a blanket from the back of the couch and wrapped it around her as carefully as I could before sitting down with her in my arms. Settled there as she was, I could look my fill and wonder at the opportunity that I found myself faced with.

I held her against my chest and relaxed, leaning back myself and remembering, until I felt her begin to stir. Then I looked down at the woman curled up and coming out of the painful high. The couch was the only piece in the room that was for comfort. Sitting on it, I thought back to the way she'd asked for more. The marks across her back would take a few days to heal. The majority would fade by morning, leaving just some light bruises behind. But a few, especially the ones at the end, would take longer. The problem with condensing my playtime into a shorter period usually meant I had to space apart the beatings and find other ways of inflicting pain in the meantime. Although I preferred impact, I didn't lack for creativity when it came to other means. Ice and heat could bring extensive pain as easily as sticks and stones. But this had been a first for me. I hadn't had a submissive that took so long to break, even a little, under the flogger.

I wondered how it was that this woman had managed to slip under my radar for so long. Had I been that obtuse or had she been just that good at hiding herself? She'd never struck me as a masochist type. Not even in the slightest. And although she was eager and had been the best assistant I'd ever had, her tenacity and confidence, and her ability to hold her own in a room full of belligerent lawyers had never indicated a truly submissive personality. Although I did know quite a few subs were successful leaders in their daily lives. Still, how had I missed this one so thoroughly? What was it about her that I seemed to have blinders on?

She stirred again and I waited. Behind my mask, I forced my features to wipe away any emotional reflections. If Danica was keeping herself a secret here, then so would I. That was, after all, my usual requirement. And perhaps I was wrong. Perhaps this woman, *Star*, wasn't actually Danica. There was a rumor that everyone had a twin, or a doppelganger. Perhaps that was who this was.

"Mmmm," her soft moan drew my attention back to her full lips.

Fuck me, I thought. I couldn't kid myself. I knew this was Danica as surely as I knew my own name. And beneath that sweet ass of hers, with just a blanket covering her delectable and now bruised flesh, was my cock. Hard and aching to sink into her softness. But not yet. I didn't cross that line until the third or fourth days. Always with extra care and precautions, but also to ensure that the woman I chose did in fact enjoy the levels of pain I needed to give. If she didn't actually enjoy the pain, which was perfectly common as well, then I wasn't going to waste my time.

To some that probably seemed exceptionally cold and calculating, but for me, it was necessary. I didn't give myself much time to be the sadist. Ten days, twice a year, was all I had. And until now, it was all I thought I'd needed.

She stirred again, this time her eyes blinking open and looking up at me, clear and coherent.

"You are a true masochist, aren't you?" I asked her, not bothering with platitudes.

She nodded and sighed, shifting and forcing me to release my hold so she could settle on the couch beside me. She held onto the blanket and wrapped it around her tightly. Her cooling flesh probably meant she was beginning to feel cold.

"Most of the women I've had sessions with before fall into a headspace with the light burning. It took much more for you to reach that enjoyment."

I waited, watching her closely for any information she might give away with a look or an expression.

She shrugged her shoulders. "I don't know why, if that's what you're asking."

"It was a statement, not a question. But there is certainly curiosity," I admitted.

"I can't satisfy that either," she retorted.

"Has it always been like that?" I asked.

She nodded. "The first time I experienced impact play with a partner, I grew bored. The guy was determined to keep going though. We met twice more, trying different things because I was new and didn't know what I might like or not like. It was the third session that he snapped. He got angry because I wasn't responding the way he wanted. He started to take it out on me and I felt the difference immediately. But, because of how he was doing it, I called my safeword and the monitors who were already concerned, pulled him off me."

I felt the anger simmering in me at her words. Though it was obviously behind her and she'd done the right thing to end the play, it stirred something dangerous in me to think that someone had taken anger out on her in a session that was meant to be controlled, safe, and sane.

"After that, I looked into more extreme players. Ones that enjoyed exerting strength over finesse. I didn't want palm prints that would disappear in a few hours. And even the lighter paddles made my skin burn, but it wasn't enough to make me lose my head or anything. I've seen plenty of subs go into that space. Some get giggly, some get quiet, they're all different except for one thing. All of them relax. I've seen it. I've never really experienced it myself though. Not like they do. My body wants the pain and by the time I feel it the right way, I go under from it instead of being able to enjoy it for an extended time."

She shuddered a little, her body cooling the longer she sat still.

"Come, your items will be in your room now. I want you to take a bath and relax for an hour. Then you can join me for a late dinner." I stood and held my hand out to her.

She looked startled at the sudden orders, but she took my hand and I pulled her to her feet. I needed her to rest and recover a little. I wanted to talk to her more, see if I could give her that pain in a way that let her drop the load she carried.

"At least thirty minutes soaking in the bathtub," I directed her. "There's special oils you can add to the water that will help ease the soreness. I know you want lasting pain, but we have nine more days together to enjoy it. If you allow those wounds to go without any treatment, we won't get to play as soon."

I could see that she paused to consider my words and knew I had guessed correctly. I wondered if she'd ever come to work with healing marks beneath her clothes. Those silky blouses could conceal just about anything, especially if she wore one of her suits. The well-cut jackets would not allow even a glimpse of a mark. Perhaps the days when she wore slacks instead of skirts?

I stopped. If I continued down that train of thought, I would drive myself crazy. Instead, once she was behind the door, I went to my own room. The private space allowed me to strip away the simple mask and drop the facade I used.

It was always a facade. In Miami, I was the lawyer. Around my family, I was the heir. To my friends, I was one of the guys - rich enough and known enough to get access to clubs and parties and women. Even if I didn't go for them myself. Even on St. John, there was a facade. Here, I was the sadist. Sir S. A man whose control was in his delivery of pain that bordered pleasure.

No one saw every side. No one saw beyond the facade I allowed them to see. That's how it needed to be. How I needed it to be.

SECURING HIS STAR

An hour after I'd closed the door behind her, I heard it open. The food I'd been preparing was just a charcuterie board with sliced meats and cheeses, some fruit, and a few different kinds of crackers. Light enough to eat late and filling enough to satisfy the hunger I was sure she felt. Even if she hadn't felt the pain in the way she should have, her body had expended energy during the whole session. She needed the nutrients. Which was why I pulled a few bottles of flavored water from the fridge when I heard her door. The water was enriched with additional nutrients and electrolytes. The LP was very specific in the things they kept stocked for guests.

She wore the same mask as before, a lace decorated black that made her eyes pop. But now her clothing was much more comfortable and although it didn't conceal her curves, it did hide her flesh from me. "You did this?" she asked, easing onto one of the stools that sat on the other side of the kitchen island.

"It's not exactly difficult to slice some cheese and pepperoni," I said wryly. I lifted the board and set it closer to her so she could reach easily. Then I handed her one of the bottles of water.

I watched as she took a long draw of the cool liquid and wondered if she'd ever played with extreme temperatures.

I finished slicing the last of the melon I had in front of me and added the pieces to the board before gathering the rind and seeds to discard. "I wasn't sure what you would prefer, so I put a little bit of everything I could find on the board. We can discuss food items as we eat and I'll inform the hotel to send down supplies as we need them."

After washing my hands and wiping the counter, I took the stool beside her and grabbed a handful of grapes.

She continued to pick at the tray. Trying one thing at a time, she worked her way clockwise from where she'd begun.

"Is it satisfactory?" I asked after long moments of her silence.

She paused, mid-reach, and looked up at me.

"The food, I mean," I clarified.

"Oh, yes." She paused, stumbling a little in her answer. "It's fine."

"Is there something else you would prefer rather than this?" I pressed.

She frowned. "I don't know. I didn't really consider that I would need to make my own food each day."

"Were you planning to eat at the hotel frequently?" I asked. Most guests did stay in the hotel rooms, which didn't have the kitchen accommodations that the cottages had.

She shook her head. "No, but I was thinking it would be easy things. Like peanut butter and jelly or fruit. Stuff like that."

"You had a cottage," I remembered.

She nodded. "It was nice. Not nearly as big as this one. And the living room was definitely more traditional."

"No sex swings hanging from the ceiling?" I asked.

She shook her head, but I saw the hint of a smile. She hadn't smiled since I'd seen her walk through the door. I wondered why. Did she have nothing to smile about? Or perhaps, like myself, she wasn't quite free to be herself. Even in the place where everything should have been perfect.

"I don't believe I have the makings for peanut butter and jelly right now. But if that is what you would like, I will have them deliver it. Do you have a flavor you prefer for the jelly?"

"Strawberry. Jam if they have it. Or, if you would allow it, I could request the items I had originally ordered for myself be moved over here. Much less wasteful, I think."

She looked at me and I realized that she was asking for permission. The contract hadn't overly specified what behaviors I expected outside of playtime. That was due to the fact that I rarely interacted with the women extensively. I found myself wanting to hear her ask permission for more. For the moment though, I nodded.

"Yes, that would work. You can call in the morning." I kept my tone even, controlled. "Tell me a little more about your experiences with pain."

She looked at me in surprise. I could see it in her eyes, a startled look like a deer caught in the headlights of a vehicle on a dark road.

"You mentioned earlier that you've had a crop used, as well as some other impact instruments. Have you had anyone deliver pain in a different manner?"

"Specifically, I've experienced nipple clamps and forced orgasms with overstimulation. A Wartenberg wheel a few times, but it didn't do anything for me." She shrugged and took a bite of the cheese cube in her hand. "I enjoyed the cane the most, I think. The partners I've had aren't sadists, or at least that part is secondary to the Dominant part. No one at the clubs I've gone to identifies first as a sadist. The pain that they deliver isn't at the level that I need because it's secondary to them. More like a service rather than a passion."

"Have you ever played with the same person more than once?" I asked. She was putting her submissiveness into a box away from the masochist. I hadn't heard her reference anything about ceding control. It was all about pain for her.

She shook her head. "Not really. Not since trying to find someone to provide the levels of pain I need. Before that I tried a few times with a couple people. But there wasn't much chemistry to mix with the S & m."

My mind spun with ideas. But they wouldn't necessarily work without first determining if she was as much a submissive as the vibes she was giving off. Was she just a masochist looking for pain? Or were the hints I kept getting the true woman hiding behind a desire for pain without the emotional links?

I needed to think. I needed to be sure of myself. Because testing her, stripping her of the facade she'd built into place to protect herself, would require much more than removing the veil of masochism. It would require dropping all the masks in play - mine and hers.

CHAPTER FIVE

~DANICA~

I continued to nibble on the fruit and cheese that Patrick had prepared. I hadn't actually expected that from him. Perhaps it was because I'd seen the meals he ate with clients and colleagues. Those meals were what you expected of a high-powered attorney. Steaks, seafood, drinks that were worth more than the clothes I wore. He never skimped on the five course opportunities to impress or celebrate. But this wasn't anything like that. It was casual, in a sophisticated way. But still, meat and cheese and fruit was simple. And I'd never known this man to be simple in anything.

"May I ask you questions too?" I asked. I hadn't seen anything in the contract that said I couldn't ask, but there was a paragraph that specified keeping everything professional over personal. While physical interactions were possible, there would be no further communications beyond the ten days. And no sharing of identifiable information was to happen either.

He nodded. "But I may choose not to answer."

"I understand. I'll not ask for anything that would reveal who you are. I was simply curious about how you learned you enjoyed this. The pain, I mean." I couldn't quite bring myself to ask if he'd ever been with someone more than just for play sessions. That felt like too much. In the seven years I'd known him, I'd never seen him in a relationship of any sort. The gossip around the firm didn't have anything juicy on him either. It was all speculation. His dates to events were never the same unless it was family. Cousins and siblings seemed to constantly use each other for their plus ones. I guess that was one way of getting out of having to find a date. Or being splashed across the gossip pages.

"It was a bit of an accident, actually," he said. "I went to a party in college that got a little out of hand. Somehow, I got turned around and ended up in the wrong place at the right time." He shrugged, but didn't elaborate further.

I took another bite of a cheese cube. I had a weakness for cheese. One that had led to the rather excessive curves I couldn't get rid of if I tried.

I stifled a yawn, but after a moment I felt it building again.

"Sleep," he said, pulling the board of food out of my reach. "We'll have plenty of time for questions and other things in the coming days. I'll clean up tonight, I do not want you to set any alarms. You are to sleep until you wake or until I wake you."

I nodded, standing and taking a deep breath. Before I left the room, I lifted my gaze to his. Those eyes that I could feel gazing into my soul were as sharp as ever. "Thank you, Sir," I said softly. I waited until he nodded in acknowledgement. I saw the flash of appreciation cross his face before I turned and walked to my room.

Shutting the door behind me, I pulled the mask from my face and let it fall to the floor, forgotten for the moment. I couldn't lean backwards, so I forced myself to walk the few feet to the bed and carefully crawled onto it to lay on my stomach. I could feel the stretch and pull of my skin where the lashes crisscrossed and while the burning sharpness was welcome as it occurred, the discomfort of the inevitable itching that came when healing began wasn't far off. For the moment, I could enjoy the heat that still radiated from the marks and the soreness that made me smile.

Sleep came quickly, the release of emotions plus the physical exertion had left me exhausted. Once that exhaustion hit, it was a simple matter of closing my eyes and letting the dreams come.

~*~*~*~*~*~*~*~

The next few days passed with too much speed and not nearly enough pain. Floggers, crops, canes, clamps, and even a few

SECURING HIS STAR

paddles. Each one was designed to provide maximum impact and he used them with unerring accuracy that left me in a sobbing, drained, and needy mess. It was ecstasy and as much as I felt myself falling for the sadist, it was hell to consider the reality of what might come when it ended. When the third paddle in as many days broke while he used it on my bruised ass, I almost moaned in disappointment.

His strokes were sure and fell with a steady beat that pulsed as unwaveringly controlled and constant as the blood running through my veins. I felt the pain, like a hot compress bleeding heat into my pores and pushing deeper than the surface. And it was everything I wanted and more.

"What do you say, Star?" he asked, coming into my line of sight and lifting my face with a hand beneath my chin.

Strapped as I was to the spanking bench, I couldn't do much beyond moving my head. But I could still speak. Even when my throat was becoming raw from the tears that clogged it on an endless cycle. "More please, Sir," I rasped. I looked up at him through the tears that clung to my lashes and hoped he could see the desperate plea that raged through me. Still needing and still not touching that place that was just out of reach until it was too late to enjoy.

"I'm going to find what breaks you open and when I do, you are going to scream with such angst and pleasure that the walls will echo with it," he promised harshly.

"Please," I whispered. I wanted that promise with everything inside me. I wanted to find that place he spoke of. Find it and live in it.

"Close your eyes, Star," he ordered.

I did. With the darkness closing around me, the restraints holding me still, there was nothing I could do but listen for the sound of what was to come next. The whistle of whatever implement coming through the air was a bare second before impact on my upper thighs rocked me from painful enjoyment into screaming torment that ricocheted through my nerves and shot me into an agonizing explosion.

Then nothing.

~*~*~*~*~*~*~*~

"Star." The rough whisper came from far away, but I heard it and something in me wanted to move closer to the sound. To hear it again.

"Star." There it was. Just there. I could almost think I saw something. Some light. Then darkness again.

"Come back to me." The voice whispered, coaxing me closer. Closer to…what?

The grey light faded again into black. Except I didn't disappear this time. There wasn't total silence or lack of all senses. I could hear something. Water? And a tingling in my skin. It itched at first. Almost imperceptible. But there.

"I need you to wake up for me, Star. You have to open your eyes." That voice again. It was clearer now. And closer.

"Star." And harder.

"Wake up."

I struggled to obey the order. I needed to obey. I needed to because…. I frowned. I couldn't remember what I needed to do.

"Star." There was some relief in the tone this time. "Come on now. I can see you coming back a little. Open your eyes for me."

I felt the urge again. This time, sensation came with the desire to obey. Warmth first, then a stinging discomfort. I felt the muscles of my face pull into a grimace as the world became clearer.

"Keep coming, Star. Open those eyes for me."

I took a deep breath. Water was all around me. Except I was leaning against something hard and hot. I tried to open my eyes just a bit, but the light was so bright. Everything seemed to bounce the beams straight into my eyes. I turned my head into the heat instead. Darker again. My eyes covered a little more.

"I can't turn off the sun, but can you at least speak so I know you're awake again?"

Sir. Patrick. The voice in the darkness. I shook my head. Or I tried to. It was so hard. My body was sore and the skin overworked from so many hours of play. Hours of pain. The tenderness was deep; I knew it would fade with time. But while the pain that came from the individual strikes was welcome, there was a point when the soreness was no longer a joyful reminder. The healing skin would no longer hold onto the aches, giving way to stiffness and then itching. Then healed but still colorful. Eventually the colors would fade too and all that would remain would be the memories of our time.

Memories that would need to last me a lifetime. Or longer.

I inhaled deeply and tried to find the calm inside me that had kept me steady whenever I needed it in the past. The steadfast and responsible survivor. The one that could be counted on to know what needed to be done and do it. Just then, I needed to be aware of myself enough to not let something slip. Secrets lay between us and I couldn't speak them if I tried. Not if I wanted to maintain my life as it was. I hadn't considered it before; not really. But I had certainly thought about it in the last five days. The risk in getting what I wanted, the risk in revealing who I was, it was so much higher than I had grasped before.

His hand rubbed along my side. A soothing motion that would have lulled me back into the darkness if my mind had allowed it. But instead, I thought. I imagined.

There were so many possibilities. Positive ones. Negative ones. Betrayal and harm done to me, my career, my friendships. Or a lifetime, even a short few months, of a partner in the truest sense of the word. Someone who would balance my needs with his. Someone who would claim me as his own. Someone to come home to in the evenings. Someone to lean on when I needed to stop being strong. Just having that would be an amazing adventure. But to have that with someone whose sadistic fantasies could feed me so thoroughly that I might thrive from the pain was a dream that I believed to be impossible. Even with the proof before me of our compatibility in kinks.

Somehow, I just couldn't drop the mask.

My fingers lifted to the lace still on my face. Every part of me had been bared to this man. Every inch of my body was his to command. And still, I was hidden.

"How are you feeling?" His words rumbled under my cheek.

"Sore. Hot. Good." I spoke softly, but even with the slight hoarseness of my voice, I was clear. Concise.

"Good. You were out for longer than you have been before."

"How long?" I asked.

"It's been a few hours."

My eyes opened at that. I'd never passed out for longer than a few minutes. Maybe a half hour at most. But hours? That wasn't like me at all.

"We're going to take a break for a few days and let you heal more. Your body can take a beating, but it's been almost a week straight of them. Your black marks are overlapping now and your skin is broken in more places than I'm okay with for another session."

"How long?" I asked, feeling dejected.

"We'll see how you are in the morning. I've arranged for us to have some time at the hotel this evening. In one of their private dining rooms."

"Okay. When is that? Evening, I mean."

"It's a few hours away still. Now that I know you're awake and aware, I want you to continue to rest. You can lie on the couch in the living room if you wish. Or there are the hammocks out here on the back patio that you could relax in."

"I think I want to stretch out in my bed for a little. And remove the mask," I told him softly.

He nodded. "Let's get you dried off and settled. I want to put some cream on your back and legs too."

Taking a deep breath, I let him help me stand up from the water and his lap. The hot tub on the secluded back porch was half in the shade from the palm trees and ferns on the side of the cabin, but still in the sun as well which kept the warm waters even hotter from the bright rays. He climbed out first, then offered me his hand and helped me to the deck. I winced at the soft towel that brushed over my back like sandpaper. The good pain wasn't outweighing the bad at that moment. The headspace of need had faded away with the darkness that had held me captive.

CHAPTER SIX

~PATRICK~

I had to find a way to help her reach the extraordinary level of pain that she needed for release without losing her to the inevitable fainting. I'd tried almost every instrument I had in my arsenal and even broken a few on her ass. From paddles to clamps, canes to whips. She loved every moment of the torture; I could see that. She dripped with desire and her final screams always came with an orgasm that shook her body like a tambourine and made me revel in the music that emanated from her so viscerally.

But it wasn't quite right. After the fifth day, when her screams had abruptly ended, as they usually did, but her revival took longer than it should have, I called a halt. While she rested, I researched. Most of my play partners throughout the years had preferred impact play with some mild tortures like nipple clamps or clothespins, many enjoyed orgasm control that left them hurting for more and then begging to stop. But not Dani. She truly was a Star. The kind of masochist that could take the beatings like they were love pats and still beg for more.

And I wanted to give her that more.

While she slept in the afternoon on the second day of our break, I called the hotel.

"Good Afternoon, Sir S. How are you enjoying your stay this time?" Lance greeted, the slight arrogance in his tone told me he knew what he was asking about.

"Lance, you have found a masochist that has me challenged."

"Oh?" I could hear the man's ears perk up at my admission. "Do tell."

"You know I don't like to reveal too much of myself, Lance," I scolded.

"Oh, pish. You and I both know that *I* know everything. So let's move past that. Mmkay?"

I rolled my eyes. "Do you want to help me or should I go back to the internet?" I asked.

"Oh, heavens, no!" He sounded affronted by the suggestion. "That monster of a world wide web will tangle you up in so many lies and it would be an utter disaster for you. No, no. Please, no. Ask me your questions."

I held back the chuckle that threatened as he spoke. Clearing my throat, I asked the question I hadn't yet been able to answer. "How can I bring a high level of pain to my sub without causing her to overload from the sensory extremes? I want to provide her with that high she's seeking without the overuse of her body."

And it was a body that was made for the kind of beatings I liked to give. But she also had a much higher breaking point. If I could open her up with something else, maybe I could also help her to let go of her need for staying in control of herself and aware of her surroundings for so long.

"Oh, I can help with that," Lance promised, then proceeded to outline a number of options that were either outright vetoed or appealing. After a lengthy discussion that took time to consider the options I had and the need for some privacy to set up a play area, we settled on one thing that I was looking forward to enjoying with her. "Do you have a preference of when?" Lance asked before we ended the call.

I considered it briefly. Her back had started to heal and the bruises, while still prominent, were beginning to change colors across her skin. "Tomorrow afternoon should be a good time," I told him.

"I'll make the arrangements. You just need to get her there."

"That I can do. Thank you, Lance." I meant it sincerely. The man, despite his exuberance and machinations, was one of the people who represented the best side of the Lifestyle. And he knew how to be discrete when it was needed.

After hanging up the phone, I went to check on the woman who had somehow worked her way under my skin in the short week here. A woman that had already worked her way into my heart despite my best attempts to keep her out of it.

She was still asleep. That was a blessing. Neither of us seemed to do well with the downtime between play. She was quieter than I was used to her being. I wondered if that was because she was trying not to seem familiar. Of course, there was also the possibility that she really didn't know who I was. I had learned that this was her first visit to the island and the resort, so it made sense that she would stay a little reserved when the conversations needed to remain anonymous.

I let my gaze travel over the soft curves that made my mouth water. She was voluptuous in the way that was soft and inviting. Her body was made for me to break her open. All that thickness. I hadn't broached the subject with her about taking our sessions into a carnal direction. Not that it hadn't crossed my mind more than once about how it would feel to sink into her soft body and fuck her while my marks crossed her flesh. But her breaking points had never opened up the possibility of taking it to that level. I wanted her raw and open to me if I was going to be inside her. Not passed out and unable to enjoy it with me.

Some men and women might go for that kind of thing, but it wasn't for me.

She was though. I was becoming more certain of that with each day and each play we'd had. And it really made me wonder how she had slipped by my radar for so long. My only reasoning that seemed solid was that she had not learned about her preferences until after she had become an associate. If she'd been involved in the Lifestyle while she was my assistant, I might have picked up on something. Or at the very least, that was what I was telling myself to explain away the missed details of my personal admin.

More than once, my mind had betrayed me with fantasies of things I could have enjoyed and now wanted to enjoy with her.

The opportunity to bend her over my desk after a long day at trial, tying her into place with a few ties and use a crop on her ass before fucking her pretty lips until tears fell from her eyes was now a fantasy that burned into my brain with much more detail than I'd had before.

I left the room before the urge to wake her up overcame my common sense. The masks were in place for a reason. The reason was becoming less important by the minute. I would have to decide soon if I was going to reveal myself to her or not before the end of my vacation. There were only three days left, after all.

Three more days to enjoy this woman so thoroughly that it satisfied me for a long time to come. Because being with someone

SECURING HIS STAR

so deeply masochistic had ruined me for any potential partners in the future.

One more day, I reminded myself. One more day and then I would see what came from giving her that opening she needed to reach her subspace.

CHAPTER SEVEN

~DANICA~

The soft knock at my door woke me from the fantasy that had suffused my dreams all night. I could feel the wetness between my thighs, my panties soaked from the thoughts that had run rampant through my subconscious. But it was the rough timbre of the voice that called out that had my stomach twisting into a delicious knot and my body flushing with heat and need.

"Star," Patrick's voice called from the other side of the door.

Star. I wondered for a moment if he would choose to call me that if he knew the truth. But I shook off the thought as my mind continued to wake from the fantasies and recognized the soreness that was much more prominent than it had been when I'd fallen asleep. The heat of burning pain was gone, only a brief twinge from the welts I guessed were harsher.

"It's nearly beyond a reasonable breakfast hour," he said.

I almost laughed at the conversational tone he used. In the office, he would have been supremely put off by anything that wasn't as it should be. Breakfast was meant to be served by nine if he was in early and it was needed. Looking toward the windows, I could see that the sun was already well above the horizon. "What is a reasonable breakfast hour?" I asked, raising my voice enough to be heard beyond the door.

"It's past ten," he answered.

I couldn't remember the last time I had slept so late. Carefully, I stood and walked to the door. I stooped to pick up the mask that sat on the bedside table. Securing it, I opened the door and found myself staring at the man who made my knees weak. His mask was in place as well, not that I'd expected less.

"I'll need a few minutes, Sir" I told him. "Should I be dressed in any specific manner this morning?" I asked. After two full days of resting and no play, I wasn't sure what to expect this morning.

His gaze took in my appearance. I'm sure my hair was messed up and the bruises still visible from our scenes despite the downtime. "No clothes. You may wear a robe while we eat, but I want you bare beneath it."

I nodded, my stomach twisting in anticipation. "Yes, Sir."

"Fifteen minutes, Star." His tone was hard now. A command.

I nodded again, understanding that I was being given a task and wondering if this was a test of some sort. I closed the door and pulled the mask from my face again. I had left my hair in the braid he'd continually demanded. But now my hair was a mess, pulling from the tight plait and sticking out at odd angles around my face. I undid the tangle of a braid as I walked into the bathroom. Running through my morning routine, I quickly washed my face and brushed my teeth, moving with an ease I hadn't had for a few days. Then I pulled a brush through the dark strands until no knots remained. He hadn't specified how to wear my hair, but I didn't guess he would want it loose. I tied it back at the nape of my neck instead. If he wanted it back in a braid, I could do that quickly. I grabbed the robe I'd brought with me, although it didn't conceal much since it was intended to be an added accessory to the little sheath nightgown. Before pulling it on, I turned and looked over my shoulder into the mirror. The lines from the first night were mostly faded and the bruises had turned yellow, almost no colors in their cores. The redness paled except for the welts that still remained. My skin pulled a little along those, but not with the heady, lingering burn that I enjoyed feeling. Now it was just soreness. And a slight itch that would drive me crazy if I didn't get some witch hazel on it soon.

Fourteen minutes.

I grabbed the mask and secured it over my face once more. Taking a breath, I opened the door and joined my momentary Sir in the kitchen.

"Good morning, Sir," I greeted.

"Good morning, Star," he returned. He was standing beside the stove, once again wearing only a pair of jeans that looked like they had molded to his body. They were well-worn though and I could see that he was comfortable in them.

With his back to me, I was able to look at him openly. There was a scar on his left shoulder blade that I knew was from falling out of a tree when he was eleven. Abuela enjoyed revealing to me many of his childhood exploits. It was still an obvious scar, despite the many years since. I wondered if he ever felt residual pain from the injury. He had never mentioned it or given any indication. I let my eyes wander across the width of his shoulders. He'd carried me often during our time together. I knew he was strong; I knew he worked out as part of his regular schedule. But I wasn't exactly a small woman. Short, yes. Small, no.

"Breakfast will be ready in a few minutes. I've made us scrambled eggs with sausage and toast. Why don't you call the desk and set up for more of your food to be delivered here so the items you enjoy are readily available." He spoke deliberately. I could hear it. There wasn't a question or a suggestion in his words, it was an order.

"Yes, Sir," I answered. The last few days had depleted most of my food supplies as he had ensure everything I ate was my preference. Like I'd done that first morning, I stood to leave the room.

"I'll return in a moment, then," I said. Walking through the living room, I glanced around to see if there was any indication of what he would want to do for the day. But nothing stood out. I found the phone on a small table near the entrance and dialed the desk.

"Dani! Oh my dear, *how* is everything going?" Lance greeted.

"Good morning, Lance," I said, smiling in spite of myself. "I was hoping you could arrange for some more of the food I requested to be sent to Sir S's cottage."

"I will personally see to it, my dear," he assured me. "I suppose that means your week has gone quite deliciously well?"

"Thank you, Lance," I said. "If I need anything else, I'll let you know." I made sure to emphasize my words, hoping he would get the hint.

"Oh, I have no doubt, my sweet friend. You go enjoy yourself for your last few days and I will take care of this request just as I did the others."

I couldn't see him, but I just knew Lance had a satisfied, cat-that-ate-the-canary type of smile on his face.

"Have a good day, Lance," I said, ending the call before he could ask a question that might cause me to slip.

SECURING HIS STAR

Returning to the kitchen, I found two plates set out with a bottle of hot sauce and the smell of freshly brewed coffee filling the air.

"How did you decide on breakfast?" I asked. Having spent many of my morning meals in the office, I knew what he preferred. This wasn't it. Nor was this one of the meals he had prepared over the last few days. In fact, this was one of my favorite breakfasts. Although, when I looked closer, I saw that he had significantly less eggs on his plate than I did and more sausage as well as some bacon. Did he know?

It wasn't the first time I'd had that thought. But this was quite specific. Only so many people knew enough about my tastes to prepare my favorites.

"I only arrange for enough food; I don't have specific requests. We were running low from staying here and not having anything delivered. Eggs seemed a safe option as most people do enjoy them for breakfast," he answered. It was a lie. Maybe not a total lie, but there was no way he hadn't taken into consideration my likes while preparing the food. Otherwise, my plate would have bacon on it. I didn't eat bacon. It was one of the things that he knew well because it was an argument we'd had in the past. I looked at him closely as he moved to the coffee pot. He had to know. Had Lance said something? I'd spent the last two days doing very little except resting. Perhaps he'd made a phone call.

He poured the fresh coffee and placed the mugs beside the plates. I waited to see if he would automatically grab the cream and sugar for me. Too much sugar, a splash of cream, and a wry comment about how I didn't actually taste the coffee. That was what he did every time.

But then he asked. "Do you need cream or sugar?"

I nodded, and my heart dropped a little. After a week, he should have known. Yet, he asked just as he had each morning. "Yes, please, Sir." Maybe he'd just guessed right on the bacon.

He pulled the items out for me and set them close enough to reach before he sat beside me at the breakfast bar. "Eat it all, Star. You'll need the nourishment today."

I looked over at him, finding his eyes and the intensity in them that was directed at me. "Yes, Sir," I replied. I reached for the sugar and cream to make my coffee and took a long sip once it was prepared to my liking.

"How are you feeling this morning?" he asked.

I considered saying it was fine, but I knew he would need specifics for our situation. "My back is still a little sore mostly. There are a few welts that are still healing and are starting to itch. I need some more of the witch hazel lotion for it. The soreness isn't so overwhelming that I need to rest or be cautious."

"We'll apply the lotion after we eat," he answered. "And your thighs?"

"They are just sore. I know you were harsh, but you didn't overly abuse the skin there like on my back, so the bruises there are almost gone."

"Good. Then we'll be able to enjoy some more play this afternoon. We'll finish breakfast and I'll make sure your marks get lotioned. After that, we're going to go for a walk on the beach. I've requested one of the outdoor play areas for us to enjoy this afternoon. It also has the added bonus of a hot tub which we know will be very helpful afterwards for you."

I almost dropped my fork. While I knew there was a possibility of outdoor play, I hadn't truly considered it. I wasn't opposed to exhibitionism, although it wasn't something that got me excited either. I wondered if the area he had chosen to reserve would be open to viewing or more private. But I couldn't bring myself to ask. And if I was being truthful, I was so excited to finally have more play again that I didn't really care. "I'm sure it will be enjoyable, Sir," I responded. "I look forward to what you might have planned."

I glanced sideways and saw a smile on his face. It was dark. The kind I often saw just before he eviscerated a witness's testimony for the prosecution. It was the kind he wore when he knew he would win a case because he could tear apart the holes of the people trying to put away his clients. While many people saw the prosecution as the 'good guys' in criminal proceedings, the truth was far less black and white. And Patrick O'Shaughnessy was excellent at keeping his clients from prosecution. It might not always be accurate, but he was very good at seeding doubt and turning juries around.

Now though, that smile was directed at me for much more sinister purposes. I felt a shiver race down my spine. He was going to tear me apart. I knew it. I could feel it. It was like a palpable tension that settled around me in a vise. Clutching at me and digging in until I could barely breathe and my heart raced with anticipation.

And it didn't scare me one bit. In fact, it made something in me settle. For the first time in my journey through the Lifestyle, I felt the hint of that relaxed headspace called subspace. And it was wonderful.

CHAPTER EIGHT

~PATRICK~

After my discussion with Lance and setting up our

afternoon, I realized that Danica had blinders on and in response, I had as well. She had been very focused on almost exclusive impact play pain, which she could endure well beyond most others. I had followed suit, since it was one of my favorite ways of delivering pain. But I wanted her to get lost in the headspace she craved without losing consciousness. So while I would love to watch her back get covered in stripes from my cane again, I was saving that particular play for the final night. It would be the last marks I left on her skin and I wanted them to last long enough for the memories to suffice when I returned to Miami.

I'd almost messed up during breakfast. Not putting bacon on her plate had made her suspicious. I saw the way her eyes had narrowed just slightly when she'd looked at the bacon on my plate that wasn't on hers. I didn't typically play mind games for the sake of it, but in this instance, I needed to get into her head to find the weak spots that would allow her to open up. So I'd purposefully asked about her coffee again, like I hadn't been seeing her prepare it for a week. I wasn't quite ready to strip away the facade. It wasn't something that had ever crossed my mind until she'd stepped into that interview. And even as I knew what I wanted, it still needed to be carefully considered, the consequences weighed for pros and cons, before making a decision.

After coating the still red welts that were much fewer than they'd been with the witch hazel lotion, I'd changed my jeans for my swim trunks. Although it was unlikely I would wear them by the time we entered the hot tub, I wanted her to have the option.

Walking along the beach toward our destination, I brought up the subject that needed to be addressed before we began the scene.

"You agreed to the arrangement with the knowledge I might ask for physical intercourse. Do you have any objections to that? As it's not explicitly stated within the contract, it's a point that I believe requires additional negotiations after some time together to ensure compatibility exists." I kept my voice even and the words neutral as I would for any other negotiation.

I looked down at her as she walked beside me and waited. I knew the answer I wanted from her lips, but I also knew not to expect anything until it was confirmed.

"With appropriate precautions in place, I would be in agreement to add that into our current negotiations, Sir." She

SECURING HIS STAR

looked up at me and I swore I saw a flash of hope mixed in with the desire in her eyes.

I nodded. "Of course, protection would be used. As you are in agreement, then it will become a possibility in any scenes we do moving forward. Beginning with this afternoon. Your body will be fully mine to command unless you use your safewords. Do you understand?"

She bit her lip, but I could see the excited flare of her eyes as she nodded. "Yes, Sir."

"Good. Our play area is just ahead inside the copse of trees there." I pointed a little ways down the beach where the trees jutted further out in the sand. Potted plants added to the walls of greenery that surrounded the platform. It was large enough for small gatherings, but intimate enough for individual purposes as well. Surrounded by the ferns and trees, it allowed sound to escape but unless invited through the entrance, there was no way into the play area. "I want you to go ahead of me. When you are inside the trees, you will remove your robe and lay on your stomach on the table provided. I want you to close your eyes and relax for me." I waited until I was sure she heard and understood my instructions. "Go," I told her, my hand slapping and squeezing her ass as I spoke.

She jumped slightly at the unexpected contact, but then she was hurrying through the sand toward our destination. I stayed where I was until she reached it. I wanted her to have plenty of time to do as I'd said. And I needed her fully relaxed and ready for what I was going to do next.

When I reached the play space, I pulled the cord to release a pair of curtains that sealed off the entrance and left us fully secluded in our own little candlelit, outdoor, playroom. On one side, in the back corner of the space, was a private hot tub. Big enough for possibly six people, but intimate enough for my purposes. In front of that was a small bench with towels, lotions, and some robes laid out. On the other side was the massage table I'd requested. The table was adjustable in height and was perfectly placed for me to be able to bend her over and fuck her from behind. An opportunity I was not going to resist or waste now that it was an option. She was naked for me, her arms crossed beneath her head, her eyes closed, though I knew she was awake and waiting. To one side of the massage table was a set of drawers. I knew inside them I would find additional candles - the kind I was going to use to paint her in all the colors of the rainbow. I'd also find the condoms and lubricant, and a few sex toys. And lastly, the instrument I'd elected for her. It would come later. After I drove her high and over the ledge. She would get her pain and she would get to enjoy it, if I had my say. On the other side of the table was another, smaller, table. It held a handful of lit candles that illuminated the area. Some of them were the warming oil candles, the soy wax already melted and ready to go. Wipes and towels were nearby as needed. And the special mask. The blindfold.

I walked to the table and picked that up. "Lift your head, Star," I told her. When she did, I settled the blindfold over her lace mask. "If both are too uncomfortable, you can remove the lace one for now."

"Yes, please," she answered softly. She propped herself up a little better and maneuvered the lace mask from under the blindfold and held it in my direction once it was removed. "Thank you, Sir."

"I want you to feel again today. We're going to take a long time and build the pain up until it's all you can feel but not so overwhelming that you pass out again," I told her as I took the mask. I placed it nearby. Then I picked up one of the massage oil candles. "You have enjoyed impact, but there are other ways to create pain and sharp sensations. We're going to explore those. If anything is uncomfortable, I want to hear your safeword. I don't want to find out later that something was the wrong kind of hurting. Do you understand?"

"Yes, Sir," she replied. I waited as she settled herself back down on the table.

"I'm not strapping you in place, but I want you to stay still," I told her. I set the candle jar, warm to the touch, next to her side. Then I grabbed another and set it beside her upper thigh. I wanted the oil in easy reach and I wanted her focused on the heat from the jars.

After the candles of massage oil were placed against her body, I went to the drawers and pulled out the ten body wax candles I'd ordered, the tube of lubricant, and the vibrating anal plug. The one thing the LP had going for it was its extensive availability of sex toys and supplies. Everything from the very vanilla lingerie to the extremely sharp sadist implements was available for purchase and could be provided at a moment's notice. Pet play supplies and even adult-sized diapers for those inclined toward ABDL play were kept stocked and the hotel's store could be shopped in person, over the phone, or even on the LP Resort's intranet that was only accessible from within the resort's boundaries. And I had taken advantage of that well-stocked store.

I set the candles on the table that was now clear of the massage candles. Then I moved to the side of the table and set the lube and plug in reach. I picked up the first candle and tipped it over so the oil spilled onto Danica's ass. The large globes of her ass cheeks shifted as she was startled by the sudden liquid warmth.

"Don't move," I reminded her. I set the now empty and unlit candle to the side and ran my hands through the oils and squeezed at her ass, working the warm trails of oil into her skin so that it glistened brightly. When the trails of oil were gone, I picked up the next candle and dumped it on her lower back. This time, she only twitched at the contact, her shoulders tensing momentarily before she relaxed. Again, I rubbed the oil into her skin. She let out little sighs each time I pressed against one of the lingering welts. The next candle was used to coat her upper thighs. As I rubbed up and down the sweet curves, I dipped my fingers into the space at the apex, teasing her pussy folds so gently that I knew it wouldn't be enough to satisfy her need for force. I used a candle for each of her lower legs until she was slick and shiny. Then I returned to her back and covered the rest of the marks on her upper back and shoulders. She hummed at the pressure I applied on her welts again.

I knew it wasn't enough yet. But this was just the start. I took one of the remaining candles and dripped the wax on her ass again, but this time, I pushed my hand into the tempting line that separated her cheeks. I rubbed the heated liquid on her pussy lips and teased the tight rosebud that I was going to penetrate next. I massaged the muscles there, letting her feel my intentions without speaking them. Not entering, but putting pressure there.

"Have you had your ass fucked before, Star?" I asked roughly, my thumb pressing firmly.

"N-no, Sir," she answered, her voice catching a little.

"Have you had anything in it?" I asked, the thought of taking her virgin hole was almost enough to make me forget my plans.

"No, Sir."

"This might be uncomfortable at first then," I murmured. Picking up the anal plug - I'd chosen one that was significant to stretch her out for me - I grabbed the lubricant and coated the toy. "You can take it though," I said. "You like pain. This won't be too much but it will give you something new to endure." I pressed the tip of the plug against her anus and pressed firmly.

The warm oils had helped relax the muscles, but the toy wasn't going to slide in easily. Even coated in lube it needed firm pressure. I went slowly, listening to her little whimpers and watching her ass stretch to take the toy. When it was almost to the thickest point, I paused and pulled it back again. She sighed as her ass relaxed and closed back up. I dripped more lube onto the toy and twisted the tip of it into her until she whimpered at the pressure as I pressed it in again. Circling it around to stretch her out more as I pressed it deeper, she started to breathe harder.

"You like this, don't you, Star?" I asked.

"Y-yes, Sir," she answered me.

"Does it hurt?"

"Not hurt. Burn," she answered.

"I'm going to enjoy taking you here later," I told her. She whimpered a little in response. A needy sound that went straight to my cock and made me hard.

I stopped the swirling motion and pressed the plug straight into her ass, watching as it stretched to accommodate the size and then closed over the bulbous end, leaving only the pretty red jewel on the outside. I dipped my fingers lower between her thighs and found the soaked entrance of her pussy. I pushed two fingers into her and rubbed against the thin membrane that separated her channels. I could feel the plug and her moans told me she could too.

"You are allowed to orgasm as many times as you can today," I told her as I twisted my fingers inside her and fucked her pussy with a few strokes that were fast and hard, the heel of my hand hitting the anal plug with each stroke. "You aren't quite there yet, but you will be," I said, pulling my hand from her before she got close. I pressed and held the little jewel to activate the vibrations. Then I moved away from the temptation of her ass and pussy.

I used the wipes to wash my hands of the oils and her juices. I needed to be able to grip the wax candles without fear of dropping them. I wanted her to hurt and burn the right way only.

Picking up the first candle, a bright red, I lit it with one of the flames on the candles designed only for lighting. I held the candle in one hand over her back and the other hand I stroked the soft strands of her hair. I could feel the tension in her body that was building with the endless vibrations of the plug in her ass. There were still a few massage candles leaning against her side, providing that warm heat. As I watched, the candle in my hand grew to a liquid at the tip next to the flame and a few moments later, the first drop fell.

Her body arched and she flinched at the new heat that hit her back. The oil would make it easier to release from her skin later, but for now, I was going to paint her like a canvas until she was covered with the wax and feeling pain from a stinging heat that would burn as it hardened and last through the impact I intended at the end.

"That's it, Star," I murmured as her body began to shake. Her flinching response ended just after the wax began to drip steadily in the line I drew down her spine. "Come apart for me."

She gasped now with each new drop that hit her skin until it was almost a constant noise that rose around us, filling the air with her soft cries as well as the scent of sex and heat. It wasn't a full break, but she was now, finally, riding the rollercoaster of pain that she needed.

I let the wax drip continuously onto her skin, dragging the candle in a line up and down her spine, not touching her ass just yet but staying on her back alone. When the flame had burned down to just above my fingers, I blew it out and set it in the little metal tray that was for that purpose.

I waited to pick up the next candle until she calmed down and her body settled from the shaking. Then I picked up the orange one and lit it. I didn't speak. I didn't even touch her this time. I just waited and watched. I knew she wanted to speak, but she pressed her lips together and visibly forced her body to relax. And then the wax dripped again. She cried out, flinching again at the first drop of liquid fire that hit her. A little moan escaped on the heels of it as the next drop hit her. I didn't go in a line this time. Instead, I let it hit randomly around her back. Her body flinched and twitched and her cries grew louder and longer. I didn't wait for this one to burn out before I lit the yellow candle. The orange was half gone when the yellow was dripping onto her flesh too. Hitting her in two places kept her teetering on that edge with enough pain to keep her aware and floating as she trembled for me, so close to breaking apart completely.

As the orange candle went to the side, used up and extinguished, I picked up the green candle and this time I let the wax coat her ass. The lines, like tiger stripes, were beautifully enticing and I couldn't wait to see how her skin reddened beneath the green. She was still moaning and her body was starting to shake again as I added the blue candle and more lines to her pretty ass cheeks. When that candle was done, I paused again. Five candles remained. But my need for her to come apart for me was intense. She was shaking and ready to drop for me. I could see it in her face, the part not hidden by the blindfold. Her lips were parted, her bottom lip was red and swollen from her teeth biting into it.

Her body trembled. The high she was on wouldn't last forever and I needed to feel her shatter on my cock.

I dropped the used up candle into the tray and dug my hand into her hair as I leaned down to her and whispered roughly into her ear. "I'm going to fuck you now, Star. While your body burns up I'm going to fuck your tight pussy and then I'm going to claim your ass."

The rough promise left my lips before I could reconsider. I moved to the end of the table and grabbed one of the condoms from the drawers. Pushing my swim trunks to the floor, I kicked them to the side as I sheathed my achingly hard cock. I found the lever on the table that allowed for adjustments. Cautiously, I lowered her legs until she could touch her toes to the wooden floor.

"Hold on," I warned her. Stepping behind her, I gripped her thighs and pulled her legs wide to open her up to me. The little red gem winked from her ass and I grinned. As soon as she came apart, I would break her even more by taking that virgin ass.

I pushed into her drenched pussy and as soon as I was seated to the hilt, I shifted my grip to her hips and held her tight as I fucked her with the pent up need I'd let build as I watched her writhe in pain and pleasure. My thumbs dug into her ass, pressing against the hardened wax and digging into her flesh so that bruises were inevitable.

I pulled her onto my cock hard and fast, feeling the wax break on her skin as my body and hers collided over and over. Her shaking vibrated through me and every part of her tensed until I could barely withdraw from her clenching pussy. She was burning me up and gripping me so tight that I almost lost my control. I refused to find my release before I got inside her sweet ass though. I reached one hand forward and gripped the thick locks of her hair in a fist. I pulled her up, arching her back and forcing my cock deeper into her greedy little pussy.

"Come for me," I growled at her, yanking at her hair again, giving her another pinch of pain.

She whimpered and her hands reached back over her head to wrap around my neck. Her fingers tangled in my hair too and I leaned forward, my teeth sinking into her shoulder.

I felt her whole body pause for the barest of seconds before she screamed and her body exploded into such a violent motion that I almost lost hold of her as her release swept through her. I released her shoulder and watched with unabashed enjoyment as she tumbled over that edge for me. I lowered her back to the table as she continued to shake, releasing her hair and leaning back. I let my hands grip and rub her ass. The wax broke beneath my hands, some of it flaking off while the rest stayed glued to her skin still.

I pulled from her body, smiling at the little whimper that escaped her when I did. I pulled the last of my surprises from the drawers behind me before I returned my attention to the plug that still filled her ass, stretching her for me to play with. She would still feel some pain, but it would be enjoyable. For both of us.

I set the glove I had pulled from the drawer to the side and moved to the side of the table. My hand rubbed softly up her back, feeling the bumps of wax and the heat that still infused her skin from the play. I leaned down and pressed a kiss to her shoulder, where I could see a bruise forming from my teeth digging in.

"What do you say?" I asked her. I wanted her ass and I would get it. But I needed to make sure my Star was still in that headspace too.

"More please, Sir," she murmured. Her voice was so soft and languid, I wondered if she was even truly cognizant. It was the first time I'd heard that tone from her and it was as beautifully languid as I'd imagined it could be.

"What color are you, Star?" I asked. Double verifying her ability to reason was necessary. I wanted her floating and happy in her pain, but I needed to know she was fully capable of calling a halt too.

"Green, like your eyes," she answered, a smile playing across her lips. "Such pretty eyes. I've always liked your eyes, Sir."

She was dangerously close to admitting she knew who I was, but I also noticed that she didn't say my name. She was still only calling me 'Sir.' And the truth was, I enjoyed that title from her a little too much more than I should have.

"Your eyes are beautiful too, Star," I told her. I pulled my mask from my face and let it fall to the floor. My decision was made the moment I knew she could handle the pain. I'd just chosen to put off the inevitable. But not now. I wanted her to know exactly who it was that was taking her to the highs she needed. And fuck if I didn't want to keep her after this trip was over too. I reached for the blindfold that hid her deep brown eyes from me and pulled it away.

CHAPTER NINE

~DANICA~

I blinked at the sudden light where there had been nothing but darkness and feelings. When my vision cleared, I wasn't looking at a masked Patrick. It was all of him - no mask, no facade, no *clothes*. My heart stuttered. He knew. I was still floating in a place that felt both painful and pleasurable and suddenly he was there too.

"Patrick," I whispered. I couldn't even hear my voice over the rush of blood in my ears.

"When I take your ass, I want you to know exactly who it is that's filling you up and making you scream," he said.

His hands cupped my head and his fingers twisted in my hair, gripping it painfully as he pulled my face to his and kissed me. It was the first real kiss. A claiming. And it was harsh and hungry and brutal. My hands wrapped around his wrists, holding on tight as he took my mouth with such force that I couldn't breathe and I didn't want to either. He pulled away as abruptly as he'd taken me in the first place. His hands loosened and one

SECURING HIS STAR

dipped away to cup my chin, forcing me to look up at him, to meet those Irish eyes of his that gleamed with intent.

"Who am I, Danica? Who am I to you?" he asked roughly.

"Sir," I breathed into the space between us. My lips moving before my mind could even comprehend the question.

"Good girl," he replied. "I have one more surprise for you, sweet Star."

I wasn't sure what that meant, but I nodded. His surprises this afternoon had shattered me so completely already. I hadn't ever felt pain so wonderful for so long before. It was exhilarating. I could still feel the skin on my back prickling with heat and stinging as the wax cracked and pulled, reminding me what he had done to me. *For* me.

I felt his hands on my flesh again. Rubbing over the thick wax that he'd used on me, pulling at the skin and giving me another level of pain again.

"Close your eyes, Danica," he ordered.

I sighed, letting my eyelids fall and plunging me back into the darkness where the only thing that existed was the sensations he gave me. *Him. Patrick. My Sir.*

The tug on the plug that still vibrated inside me woke my nerves up as the thick bulb that he'd pushed into me earlier was eased out.

"Your ass is mine, Star," he told me. "Only mine." I felt the head of his cock, so thick and big in my pussy and feeling even bigger now as he pushed the head into my ass that felt empty after the plug was gone. It wasn't empty anymore. I cried out as he pushed deeper.

"Oh," I cried out, my body stretching for him and my hands clenching at the sides of the table I lay on. The burn was more than I could imagine. The plug hadn't been as long. It hadn't pushed as deep. It had been a precursor. And this was so much more. "Please, Sir," I gasped as he pulled back out briefly and pushed in again.

"Please what, Star?" he growled.

"More please, Sir," I answered, giving him the words he needed. The words *I* needed.

"My little masochist," he responded, chuckling darkly. "I have more for you," he promised.

And then I felt it. His hand fell on my ass in a harsh spanking. I knew it was his hand, because he gripped my flesh tight after the blow. But there was something more. Something stingy in his palm. Studs that dug into the wax that was still attached and ripped it away while delivering the harshest spanking I'd ever felt before.

I cried out as he pulled the hand away and wax ripped from my skin in response. My body lit up on the inside all over again. I felt the rush of desire that coated my thighs again. His cock sunk fully into my ass as he brought his hand down again. The dual sensations of burning and stinging pain, inside and outside of me, mixed together as he fucked me to the same rhythm that he spanked me. Each time more wax ripped away, he pulled out. Each thud of his hand on my flesh had him sinking back in. It was endless torture that broke me even more because he knew. *He knew.*

He sunk deep and I knew he was close to his release because he stayed inside me and leaned forward. His hand moved from my ass and I felt it settle on the spot at the top of my back, between my shoulderblades. The studs gently pressed down, not hard enough yet, but enough that I held my breath in anticipation. The hand that he'd kept bare slipped beneath my body and wrapped around me to pull me up, into an arch that was both pain and pleasure to hold.

His lips moved over the skin of my shoulder, the sore spot where he'd bit me earlier.

"I own you, Danica," he whispered harshly. "I own your pain." He pulled back and then pushed deep into my ass with such force I would have lost my footing if he didn't have a solid hold on me. "I own your pleasure." He did it again. "I own every scream." Again. "And every gasp." Again. "And every cry." Again. "Your body. And your submission. I own it all." His strokes quickened. My breathing grew more ragged. "Who owns you, Danica?" he asked, still stroking his cock in and out of my ass so hard that I was able to feel little else but his claiming of me.

"You do," I answered. "You own me, Sir," I managed to cry out the words as he pressed his studded hand tight against my back and dragged it down my spine, ripping large strips and chunks of wax from my flesh and sending me into a spiral that ended suddenly in an explosive orgasm.

"That's my Star," I heard him say as his strokes quickened and his hands gripped me so tight that I could barely breathe in his grasp. And then he groaned and I felt the jerk of his cock in my ass as he came.

He held me tight until the last tremors left us both and the world grew quiet except for the ragged sounds of our breath.

"Beautiful," I heard him say as his lips kissed a path down my back. "I wish I'd taken a picture before I ruined it."

"Next time," I murmured without thinking. My eyes were closing as my body hummed and my mind floated in a place I hadn't existed in before. Subspace. It was as amazing as I'd heard it was.

"All the next times, Danica. *All* of them," he responded. There was something in the tone of his voice that should have alerted me, but at the moment, I was too lethargic to focus.

I felt him pull out of my ass and I hissed at the loss and discomfort that hit me.

"Just relax," he murmured. "I'm not done with you yet."

I blinked open my eyes briefly to throw him a curious look. But he was out of my sight. I heard movement and he was back a few minutes later, closer again.

"I'm going to turn the table back into a full table," he said. I felt my legs lift and when the leaf was back in place, he helped me shift to a more comfortable place and picked up the pillow that had fallen to the floor at some point. He kissed my temple and played with my hair for a moment. "Close your eyes and enjoy this, Danica, my Star."

I frowned, not sure what I was supposed to enjoy. Then I felt the tug on my skin. "Oh," I murmured, humming a little at the burn/sting of pain that came from a piece of wax being scraped from my skin.

"There's still a lot on you," he said. "And I plan to draw out this pain for you as long as possible."

I felt everything settle inside me, like a cat settling into the sunlight for a long nap. And as he scraped the wax from me, I let myself float in that space. I let the burning stings wash over me and envelop me until it was like a blanket of stinging heat that held me in that space of pain and pleasure. That space that gave me everything I needed to float away and just be.

I felt the neediness building in me again as Sir continued to remove the wax. I could feel my body growing wet with desire.

Long before he finished, I was whimpering and my shifting had led to more than one smack on my ass and a reminder to stay still.

When he was done, he disappeared and I opened my eyes to look around for him. I heard movement by my feet, but he was out of my sight, even if I shifted my head to look in that direction. But then he was back, and walking toward me with his cock standing thick and hard, bobbing slightly as he moved but obviously ready for more like I was.

I licked my lips and raised my eyes to his.

"Do you need fucked again, my Star?" he asked me. "Did removing the wax make you a wet mess for me?"

I nodded, not quite daring to speak yet.

"Sit up and spread your legs. Let me see how wet you are," he commanded.

I moved as quickly as my aching body allowed. The soreness hadn't quite set back in, but it was coming. I could feel it just there, but not quite taking over yet.

I hissed in a breath as I settled on my ass though. The wax had left its mark and I could feel the sensitive skin protesting as pressure was applied.

I saw my Sir smirk at the sound. The knowledge of what was causing me pain gave him pleasure in the same way having him give me pain gave me pleasure.

I widened my legs and leaned back. The softer curves of my belly and thighs had once been a worry of mine, but his gaze eating me up pushed those insecurities into the trash.

He stopped in front of me, dropping something on the table beside me before he reached his hand between my thighs and pushed a finger into me. His other hand gripped my chin, keeping my gaze locked with his as he teased my body with just a single finger.

"I'll enjoy getting to see your eyes roll back this time," he said roughly. He pulled away and released me.

I almost pouted in frustration but caught myself in time to see him grab the condom he'd brought over and rip it open. When his cock was covered with the thin latex, he pulled me to the very edge of the table, his hands making me whimper as they gripped my wax-marked ass. I expected to feel him pull me onto his cock. But instead, he backed up another step and pulled me off the table.

He held me until I was steady, but I couldn't resist the glare I shot up at him. He dipped his head and kissed me hard, his hands rubbing up and down my burning back until I was moaning and melting into him.

"Go get in the hot tub," he told me, lifting his head.

I carefully picked my way over the wooden boards to the hot tub in the back corner. It was when the water reached just above my knees that I realized what would happen when I sat down. I turned and found him standing right behind me. He leaned down and gripped my thighs, pulling me up and into his arms. As he lowered himself to the corner seat, he adjusted me and pulled me onto his cock shortly before the hot water hit the still hot marks and sent me spiraling into a sudden and unexpectedly fast orgasm.

"Fuck," I heard him mutter harshly as he gripped my hips and pulled me closer.

I felt the heat of him as my pussy spasmed around his cock. My eyes closed briefly at the sensations that swirled through my body. Then a stinging grip of my hair and a growl brought my lashes up and I found myself staring into those eyes of his. The ones that had mesmerized me for so long and left me in an aching needy mess more nights than I cared to admit.

"Keep your eyes open," he demanded. "Who's claiming you? Who owns you, Danica?" he asked.

"You do, Sir," I answered, a moan escaping as he dragged me up and down his cock like I weighed nothing. Later I would realize that in the water, I probably weighed just about that. But just then, the feel of him and the strength of his grip on me made me lose all sense of the rest of the world.

I felt another orgasm building as the first subsided and I didn't fight it. For the first time, I let it just sweep me away and trusted that my partner would keep me safe in the storm. As my body shuddered in ecstasy, I felt him jerk and groan and then my body filled with a new warmth. I fell forward, my head resting on his shoulder as he wrapped his arms tight around me and held me close, still buried deep inside me like he belonged there.

I don't know how long we stayed like that. The hot water soothed and stung my body and I wanted to stay in that place, that feeling. When Patrick finally shifted and pulled me off him, I whimpered in disappointment. But a moment later, he had me on his lap again, sideways this time, but holding me just as close. And I let my eyes close, this time falling into the soothing darkness without the abruptness that usually happened after I broke.

CHAPTER TEN

~PATRICK~

I let her hide for two days. When I woke her after the hot tub, she'd closed in on herself. The broken condom plus the physical and emotional releases she'd experienced had pushed her into an emotional overload that I hadn't anticipated from the woman I knew to be strong, capable, and decisive. But dinnertime on the second day was where I drew my line. We had one more night to spend together before the vacation ended and I was not going to let either of us spend it alone. She wasn't alone in the shift of status quo. My world was as changed by our overwhelming scene as hers was. And I refused to let her handle it on her own or let her own mind have conversations with me that I had no knowledge of.

I knocked first. "Danica, we need to discuss this. Please open the door." I waited, listening for even the slightest movement on the other side. There was nothing. I sighed. I was not used to this. Not from anyone, but certainly not from the woman that had learned how to go toe to toe with me in order to fight her way to the top while also pushing herself down the ladder.

"Unless you use your safeword in the next five seconds, I'm coming in," I called out. I waited, counting to ten before I actually reached for the doorknob. It surprised me when it turned easily and I was able to walk right in. Except, instead of finding my submissive stubbornly avoiding me, the room was empty and the bed was made like it hadn't been slept in.

"Danica," I muttered, turning on my heel and stalking toward the phone in the hall.

"I can't believe it took you this long to call. How did you not notice that she was gone for a full day?" Lance's voice was exasperated. It was a tone I hadn't heard from him before.

"I was giving her space that she asked for," I said. "Now she's had her time and there hasn't been a dissolution of our contract. That means she is still in my service. Where is she, Lance?" I asked, my voice hardening.

"She's in her cottage, of course. Goodness, but you sadists must really be obtuse at times."

I could practically hear the eye rolling on the other end of the line.

"Lance! The cottage number."

"Oh, do be patient. If you come at her all aggressively, she is going to run right back to Miami. And she might just leave your firm too," Lance admonished. "Now take some deep breaths and then take yourself on a walk over to the Cove side of the resort. Cottage C3 would be an excellent destination for you."

I breathed deep and blew out the breath I was holding. "Thank you, Lance."

I hung up the phone as he said something about an invitation. I wasn't sure if it was directed at me, but it didn't matter. I grabbed the keys for my cottage and left, taking the most direct route that cut straight across the resort to the cottages just off the beach on the tamer side of the resort.

By the time I reached her cottage, I was calmer than I had been but still determined that she and I would discuss what happened. I knocked on the door and waited. Hearing movement inside was at least a sign of life that I hadn't had before.

"What do you want, Patrick?" I heard through the closed door.

"Unless you wish to call your safeword and back out of the contract you signed, you are under obligation to follow my rules and do as I say," I told her. "Right now, I want you to let me in so we can talk."

The click of the lock was followed by the door opening. "There's nothing to talk about," she argued, staring up at me from tired eyes.

"Are you calling your safeword?" I asked.

She cast her eyes downward and I could see the wheels in her head turning with all the arguments. Then she moved backwards with a shake of her head and I felt the weight of worry lift away. She wasn't safewording out and she was letting me in.

I closed the door behind me and flipped the lock back into place. We did not need any interruptions. It was two steps before I caught up to her, following closely as she moved into the living room. This cottage had a traditional living room, just like she'd remarked after first seeing mine. I pulled her to the couch when she would have chosen one of the chairs. After two days of not touching this woman, I needed to feel her. And I was fairly certain she needed it as well.

I sat and pulled her onto my lap. Her hair was loose and fell around her face, hiding her eyes from me. I let her keep her barrier in place for now. "Why did you leave?" I asked.

"I needed space," she answered softly. Her fingers were clasped in her lap, knuckles white with tension.

"I was giving you space," I responded. Something about the way she had drawn into herself had me worried. I couldn't quite pinpoint what it was.

"I needed more space," she argued weakly.

"Dani, we can go back and forth on this all night. It still doesn't explain why you ran away." I sighed and pulled her against me. No more holding back, no more hiding. I wouldn't let her close me out when I'd just discovered how to open her up.

"I won't be that woman, Patrick." I almost missed her words, they were so soft.

"What woman?" I asked, confused.

"I won't be the trap-a-man-into-something-because-a-condom-broke-and-I-got-pre gnant woman."

I wanted to laugh, but I couldn't. Something was behind that comment. That fear of hers. "Dani, we don't even know if there is a baby. And I think that your reaction is also coupled with subdrop. You told me you had never been in subspace before. Tell me you didn't experience it that afternoon. Can you say that?" I asked gently.

She shook her head, shrugging her shoulders too in a confused response that told me she was still going through the drop.

"My Star, I think you're still experiencing it," I said softly, rubbing her back gently. I felt her stiffen as I did so and I moved her to lean forward, lifting the loose shirt she wore so I could see her back. "Fuck, Dani. You can't reach your whole back to put the lotion on, can you?"

She sniffled and shook her head. "Don't yell at me," she sobbed.

SECURING HIS STAR

"I'm not yelling at you, Star," I assured her. I moved her carefully off my lap. "Is the lotion in the bathroom?" I asked.

She nodded, leaning forward and resting her head on her knees. I caught a glimpse of those dark eyes of her, watching me from behind her hair.

I went into the bathroom and found the lotion, taking a deep breath to calm myself down before I went back to her. I settled behind her and carefully raised her shirt again. I could see the areas she had been able to reach - the backs of her shoulders, most of her lower black, and I was sure her ass was treated since she hadn't had an issue sitting down - but the center of her back was still covered with angry reddened skin from the wax play. I coated my hands and then gently pressed them to the harshest areas first. She hissed in pain and flinched. I didn't back off until I'd coated the whole area with the soothing lotion. It would take a minute, but the witch hazel would help pull out the sting and calm the skin. I went to the kitchen and rinsed my hands. When I returned I put myself right in front of her and moved her hair out of the way. "You will not let yourself suffer like that again. Do you understand?" I said, my tone hard, unyielding.

"Yes, Sir," she answered, her lashes dipping down to look away.

Whatever was going on in her head, the fact that she was still deferring to me told me she still wanted to be in that place.

She still wanted to be mine. It was more reassuring than anything else she could do in that moment.

I sighed to myself. Sitting on the couch again, I pulled her back into my lap, taking extra care to avoid the area of her back that was still raw. "Who do you know that was that woman, Dani?" I asked carefully.

She shook her head against my shoulder, refusing to answer.

"Do you know that I have fought my attraction to you since the day I first saw you sitting at the desk outside my office?" I asked.

"What?" Her head came up and she met my eyes in suspicious surprise.

"It's true," I told her.

"But you barely said a word to me for a week. And then it was just to bark out orders and dictations. Even the recorded dictations were always terse."

"I was thirty years old and already very well aware of my preferences. And you were barely out of high school," I reminded her. "Not to mention the fact that I didn't know you well enough to know if you would run screaming to the press or file a harassment suit against me if I did pursue something."

SECURING HIS STAR

She bit her lip and frowned. "I guess that makes some sense. But that only applies to the beginning of my time. What about later? Once you knew I wouldn't do those things?"

"By then, you were the best administrative assistant I'd ever had. And you were still much younger than me. I have very carefully kept my professional and personal lives separate from my sadistic preferences. There's too much at stake if I were to be outed. Even within the local community in Miami, there's just too much risk." It wasn't that I hadn't explored it when I was younger. In fact, before taking my place in the family business, I'd gone to a number of play parties and dungeons. Once I was in the firm, though, I just couldn't risk the publicity. Not then. Not now.

"So you sacrifice part of yourself for the business?"

I shook my head. "Not like that. I still take my trips, and I have for quite a few years even before you came to the firm. But I do keep my private life exceptionally private. Too much of my life is in the public eye to begin with. Between the firm's successes and the constant charities and fundraisers Abuela makes us attend, there's really not much time anyway. Except my vacations."

"Twice a year. Ten days away and no contact." She would know, of course. "Your new assistant's theory is that you're gay and meeting your lover who you refuse to acknowledge."

I laughed. The comment caught me completely off guard, particularly with the very wry tone Dani used to deliver it. "I suppose that's not the worst thing she could come up with. Although she is partly correct about the type of getaway. She has a few details wrong though." I looked down and caught a slight smile on those pretty lips. "What did you think?"

She looked back up at me again, those dark brown eyes peering through her thick lashes. "I thought it was some kind of anti-technology disconnection retreat. You know, the kind where you can leave the constant access behind and find some peaceful quiet." She shrugged. "You always seemed much less tense afterwards, so I thought it was either that or a spa and you really didn't seem like the kind of guy to enjoy a mud bath."

I chuckled. "The trips do help relieve some tension, of course. But you're correct, I'm not a mud bath type." She smiled again. Just a little, but it was enough to satisfy me for now. She wasn't sad and fearful at the moment. "When did you find out the truth?" I asked.

She swallowed and looked a little guilty. "A little over a year ago. Maybe eighteen months."

I raised a brow, surprised. "You never said anything."

She shook her head. "I didn't know what to say. I was...intrigued, I guess."

I waited, not speaking to ask the questions that were building in my mind. I'd learned that often it was silence that was the best tool for getting someone else to speak.

SECURING HIS STAR

"Lance sent me some information for places in Miami that could give me some education on the Lifestyle and things just sort of fell into place after that."

"Did Lance tell you when to be here?" I asked. If he had set this up on both of us, I was going to be more than a little upset. The LP was exceptionally respected because of their value on privacy.

She shook her head. "No, not exactly. I knew your trip was coming. It's on the firm calendar so we know you're out of reach. I overlapped my vacation with yours and came out a day earlier." She looked down at her fingers, twisting them together again in that nervous way she sometimes had. "I did ask him for an introduction though," she whispered.

I tipped her chin up with a firm grip on her jaw. "You knew then?" I asked. "When you walked into that interview, you knew who I was?"

She bit her lip and I felt the pressure as she tried to nod. "Yes," she answered, the word barely a breath of sound above silent.

"What else did you know?" I heard my voice hardening. I didn't like to be played.

"Only that you enjoyed giving pain. Lance tried to get me to take a trip once before; he even had me fill out his questionnaire. I backed out though because I didn't feel ready. He kept dropping hints about setting me up with the perfect sadist. Never specific or even enough for most people to figure out. But I'm not the youngest lawyer in Miami at the top law firm for nothing. I knew he meant you. And he knew I'd thought about the possibility for a lot longer than since I learned about kink." She jerked her head out of my grip and tried to stand.

"No, you can stay right here until you finish talking," I told her, wrapping my arms securely around her waist to hold her still. "What does that mean? What did you think about?"

She glared at me and then looked away. "It was girlish fantasies. Nothing else."

Girlish fantasies. I hid the grin that was threatening to surface. "And after you learned about kink?" I pushed.

She flushed. From her dark roots to the tops of her breasts that I was catching a glimpse of when she shifted just right. "They weren't so girlish after that," she admitted.

"Danica," I said her name like a command and waited for her to turn her head back to me. When her eyes met mine, I continued. "Why did you arrange our meeting?" I asked.

Her eyes dipped away from mine briefly. When she raised them again, I could see the need and defiance in her flashing out at me.

"I wanted to know if Lance was right," she answered. "I wanted to know if my desire for you was or could be returned. Even a little."

"And you were willing to go through a week and a half of anonymous play and then what? Would you have ever told me the truth? Would you have been able to work with me with that between us?"

She shook her head. "I don't know. I didn't really think you would pick me even though I'm certain Lance rigged the interviews."

"Oh, he definitely did that," I told her. "But you went through with it. You read the contract. You knew what I was asking for. And you agreed."

She nodded. "I wanted to know." She shrugged. "And maybe part of me still has that girlish fantasy at the back of my mind."

"What was the fantasy?" I asked.

"That you would notice me as more than your assistant," she said softly.

"Then why did you run when I did just that?" I asked, bringing us back to the original question.

CHAPTER ELEVEN

~DANICA~

I bit my lip. How could I tell him that I'd spent years watching my mother and father constantly fighting and feeling so unloved and unwanted by both of them? How could I explain that when my father finally walked out, my mother tried the same trick with every boyfriend she brought home after him? That I had a half dozen half siblings who I'd spent so much time raising myself because the parent that I lived with was more interested in what she could get out of her next lover than in taking care of her children?

"I don't have the kind of family you have," I said. "My mother is an extremely selfish person and my father left when I was seven. He was only there because she got herself pregnant with me when they were kids themselves. She was sixteen and he was eighteen. Their parents gave them the option of getting kicked out of their homes or getting married and having help. My dad stuck around until a year after his mom died. My grandma is the only person I can remember taking care of me. When she died, everything fell apart. And my mom thought she could fix things if she got herself pregnant and hooked another husband. Except it didn't work out the way she wanted."

"So your mom is the woman you don't want to be?" Patrick asked gently.

I nodded. The barest bones of my past were still more than I usually shared with anyone. I'd fought my way out of that place. I wasn't the girl in the trailer with the threadbare clothes anymore. I didn't have six kids to fix dinner for or make sure their homework was done. The youngest of my half-siblings was almost done with high school and the others were already gone like me. I knew where, of course; I kept in touch. But we were all well past that time when life looked like the beginning of a survivor novel.

"You're forgetting something though, Dani," he added.

I frowned. I wasn't forgetting anything.

"I'm not the kind of man to be forced into anything I don't want."

I couldn't argue with that. Even on the toughest of cases, Patrick had always found a way around the obstacles to bring people to his side of things.

"*If* there was a baby, and that's a big if, then I'm just as responsible. But being a father to a child doesn't require marriage or even support from me to you except in direct regard to the care and well-being of the baby. That choice is there for any man who finds himself in that kind of situation. But more than that, I know that you aren't that kind of a person. *You* aren't even able to claim responsibility for the condoms being there, much less the unfortunate fact that one broke. You were in my care at that time. You are still in my care now. And I've known it was you from the moment you walked through that door. I knew being with you would be playing with fire. I knew it and I wondered if it was smart of me to even send the contract. But like you, I wanted to know too."

I looked at him with surprise. "You knew it was me?" I asked.

"You and I spent countless hours together in close proximity for years. Did you really expect that I wouldn't notice it was you even with that mask?"

I shrugged. I honestly hadn't thought he'd paid that much attention to me outside of what the job required. I'd never gotten even a hint from him that he saw me as more than his assistant.

"My job requires that I note every detail of every case - from the people involved to the things they say, how they say it, and what gestures or movements they make when they're talking. If I didn't pay attention like that, I wouldn't be nearly as good at my job. You are a person that I was near and interacting with daily for long hours each day. Your very way of walking into a room is something I'm acutely familiar with. And I was always watching when you walked out as well," he added.

I swallowed hard. "Oh." I felt my mouth go dry at the implications he was dropping. I didn't know what else to say. I felt so unbalanced. The emotions that had torn through me when he'd told me the last condom had broken had ripped me apart and left nothing but worry and fear building up inside me. Now, the gut-wrenching response I'd been fighting for two days wasn't nearly as suffocating. I wanted to curl up and just sleep against this man. Being in his arms, held and a little coddled even, was soothing the part of me that had freaked out so thoroughly.

I let my head fall against his shoulder and closed my eyes.

"When was the last time you slept or ate, Star?" he asked.

I like that he was still calling me Star. Like it was who I was to him. Special. His Star.

"I had some water earlier. I think I slept a little last night, but not good." I answered honestly, even knowing that it would make him upset with me. He was already upset about my back.

"You can't do that," he chided softly.

I shrugged. "It wasn't on purpose."

"Come with me," he said, setting me to the side before standing and holding out a hand.

I looked at it blankly for a moment, then slowly placed one of my hands in his. He pulled me up from the couch and led me into the bedroom.

"Sit while I grab the few things you need."

I lowered myself to the bed and watched as he grabbed the little carryon bag I had and went into the bathroom. I heard movement as he put stuff in the bag, though I wasn't sure what it was. Then he was back in the bedroom and opening the drawers to grab clothes. Not much, but at least an outfit or two. He zipped the bag closed and grabbed my sandals from beside the door and brought them to me.

"I'm going to call and have food prepared and brought to the cottage for us. After we eat, you and I are going to sleep." He slid my shoes onto my feet and looked up at me. "I'm not letting you out of my sight again for a little while," he said. "You feel anxious or worried, you don't run away. We talk about it. If you can't do that, then you use your safeword."

I felt the twisting of my stomach at his words. He was asking me for a lot more than he realized with that order. I wasn't sure if I could open up and let him in that much. But I also knew, in that soul deep way, that I didn't want to use my safeword with him. I just didn't want to end our contract when I'd only barely tasted the pain I craved. "I'll do my best," I promised. It was all I could say.

SECURING HIS STAR

He nodded, accepting my words and probably seeing right through me too. "How hungry are you?" he asked, pulling me to my feet again. He picked up the bag and set it on his shoulder as he led me from the room.

"Not very," I admitted.

"You need to eat, Dani," he said. He stopped by the phone and picked it up, calling the concierge desk.

"Dani?" Lance's voice was muffled, but I could hear it.

"No, it's Sir S. We're returning to my cottage, but we'll need some light fare sent over for our dinner."

I strained to hear what Lance answered in return, but Patrick had pressed the receiver closer to his ear and the muffled noise was just that now - noise. I couldn't distinguish the words.

"That will be fine. Please have hot and cold options available. And tomorrow, we will be packing up Dani's cottage and she will be leaving with me. You can refund her remaining days on it and make it available for another guest immediately."

My head came up at that. My cottage? I frowned and looked around. I had kept it because I didn't know how things would go. Having a place to escape to made me feel like I still had something in my control even as I gave that up to *him*.

"Lance wants to hear you say you've agreed to this," Patrick said, holding the phone toward me.

I hadn't actually agreed. Or at least, what I had agreed to didn't specify giving up my cottage. But he was my Sir. He had control of my choices just then. I knew, if I argued, I would only get out of it with my safeword. And that would open up much more than just keeping the little cottage.

"Lance?"

"Dani! Oh, sweetie. Please tell me I'm hearing this because you are going back to him willingly. He wasn't a big bully or anything, was he? So many Dominants have that stubborn tendency to just forget that they might be in charge, but that doesn't mean they can *actually* control everything. Are you okay?" Lance's words came almost too quickly that his European accent slipped a little.

"I'm okay. Or at least I'm more okay than I was," I told him. "I'm going back to the cottage with Sir S and we're going to keep talking about what happened."

"And you agree about giving up your place? Going back early?" Lance pushed.

"Yes. He has stipulated that I cannot run away when I'm upset. If I stay here, I'll be hiding." That was true. If it was bad enough that I was ready to run off the island, then Patrick might have a problem. But if the last few days hadn't chased me back to Miami, I didn't guess that anything could.

"Okay, my dear. I'll schedule a cleaning to be done tomorrow night. Now put that sadist back on the phone so I can give him the requisite friend warning."

I felt amusement as I handed the phone back, but I hadn't quite the energy to laugh.

Patrick - *Sir* - sighed and rolled his eyes as he listened for a few minutes. "Lance, I need to get her back before she falls asleep standing here."

I could tell he'd interrupted the other man's speech by the expression on his face.

"I know she needs care, Lance. That's why I'm hanging up and you will have the food delivered shortly after we get there. Right now, she needs nutrients and rest. She can check in with you tomorrow after she's had both and you'll see her before we leave."

Just before he hung up the phone, I could hear Lance muttering about "the things I go through" and I couldn't help but smile.

"You seem to have a very determined and protective friend, Star," he commented, looking down at me.

I nodded. "I know. He's been extremely helpful and a great listener over the last year and a half."

"Hmmm." He looked thoughtful, but then he took my hand and guided me to the front door. "When we reach the cottage, I want you to take this shirt off and I'll put another layer of lotion on your back."

I listened as he continued to talk as we walked. My energy was fading much quicker than I expected it to. Probably the combination of not eating and the overwhelming emotions. As we walked down one of the paths that took us through some trees, I almost ran into a couple heading the opposite direction.

"I'm so sorry!" I blurted, my focus snapping back into place as I took in the outfit of the woman I'd narrowly missed.

"It's okay," she responded. "No harm done. Are you all right?"

I nodded as Patrick came up beside me and wrapped an arm around my waist, careful of my back still.

"She's having her first drop," he explained as I leaned against him.

"Oh, honey. Food, a good long soak in the tub, and some rest is the best thing for that. Don't be afraid to cry if you feel like it either." The blonde spoke sweetly and with a genuine concern despite the pink-hued cat ears on her head and the little bell on the matching collar around her neck.

"Let's let them keep going on their way so she can do that, kitten," the tall man beside her said. "You need some food yourself too," he added.

"Oh, of course. Enjoy your stay," she said to us, giving a little wave.

As they moved past and we continued in opposite directions, I heard a vague mention of swimming to a bar. That made no sense to me, so I shrugged it off and simply leaned on Patrick for the rest of the walk to his cottage. *Our* cottage.

"Let's get some lotion on your back again before the food arrives," he said after we were safely inside.

I nodded and pulled the shirt I wore over my head. I hadn't bothered with a bra or even a cami. It had been all I could handle to have the soft cotton of my oversized t-shirt against the raw marks.

I felt my nipples tighten in the cooler air of the cottage and my arms crossed in front of me. The gesture was meant to bring warmth to that area but instead, I caught sight of Patrick's eyes dipping down and following the generous curves with a decidedly wolfish look. Suddenly, I wasn't cold anymore. The flush of desire didn't do anything to change my situation either.

My eyes dropped down and I could see the hard length of his cock pushing against the soft denim of his jeans. I shivered, memories rushing through me. The feel of his cock inside me. Especially when that fullness had been coupled with the delicious pain of the wax that he'd poured on my skin. The exhaustion I'd been feeling was slipping further away as my body responded to his appreciative perusal.

"Arms down at your sides," he told me.

It took me a moment to comprehend, but then I let my arms fall and my breasts were fully bared to his view.

He reached out with one hand and cupped one. Lifting it gently and rubbing his thumb around my nipple so softly that it barely registered except to make me want more.

Then he dropped his hand away. "Turn around for me, Star," he said.

I did as he asked, pulling my hair over one shoulder so he could see my back. I heard him open the bottle of lotion, but the cold witch hazel still startled me when it first hit my skin. He rubbed it in carefully on the center of my back. Then with a bit more pressure around my shoulders.

"Lower your pants and panties and bend over," he ordered.

I didn't protest or even sigh. I knew he would want to see it all eventually. My ass, big though it was, was still reachable. I had been able to apply the ointment several times in the last few days, minimizing the pain enough for me to handle sitting.

Still, he applied more. And the feel of his hands rubbing over my ass made me almost moan in appreciation. It wasn't the same roughness as before, but there was a tease in the gentle way he was caring for me when I knew just how harsh he could be too.

When he was done, he knelt behind me and helped me out of my shoes and leggings.

"You can stay naked for the night. Your back needs at least twenty-four hours with regular applications to diminish those marks enough for more play. In the meantime, you and I can spend some time learning about each other in more ways."

"More ways?" I asked, curious.

"Oh yes, my sweet Star. There are plenty of things we can do while your back heals up a bit."

I had questions, but we were interrupted by a knock on the door.

"Go wait for me in the kitchen," he said. As he passed me, he pressed a kiss to my hair and then kept walking to the door.

I looked after him for a moment until I heard the door open. The sound jolted me out of my confusion and I went to sit at the little bar and wait.

CHAPTER TWELVE

~PATRICK~

The early morning light woke me well before Dani. I'd given her space before, but after I'd gotten her to eat enough to give her some necessary nutrition, I'd settled her in my bed. I'd crawled in next to her and held her as she slipped into an exhausted slumber. Holding her body against mine had felt right. It was something I hadn't really given much thought to before. Having someone in my bed, spending the night with anyone, had never crossed my mind. Now, I didn't want her to leave it.

Leaning down, I pressed my lips to hers, kissing her with gentleness despite the desire I had to take with a ferociousness that had nothing to do with being gentle. I reigned it in though. Because what I wanted just then was to consume her so completely that there was no doubt in her mind that she was meant for me. That I was the Sir she needed in her life.

Slowly I felt her respond. Her body came alive beneath my hands as I ran them over her curves. Squeezing softly, pinching a little to draw gasps of surprise. When she moaned and her fingers

SECURING HIS STAR

came up and sunk into my hair, I knew she was awake. When her body shifted and her legs parted for me, I knew she wanted more.

"Turn over," I whispered, pulling back and releasing her as I reached to the bed stand and grabbed a condom from the drawer.

She shifted and I watched as she got into position for me. I sheathed my cock with the latex and grabbed the lube that was there as well.

"Spread your legs, Star," I told her.

She obeyed and I moved to kneel between the thick thighs that I was ready to feel wrapped around me.

"Bring your knees under you," I told her. "I'm going to take your ass again."

I watched the shudder that rippled through her as she complied. When her ass was right where I needed it, I slapped it hard. Her moan echoed around the room and she leaned backwards, pushing her ass into my hand.

"Who owns you?" I asked her.

I opened the lube and squirted some onto my fingers, pressing against the tight rosebud that I wanted to sink into again.

She shifted as she answered. "You do, Sir." Her tone was light and soft. I could hear the anticipation in her voice mixed with a growing need.

"I'm not going to be gentle," I warned her.

She looked back at me over her shoulder and the flash of desire that filled them told me she didn't want gentle either.

I pushed one finger in, not bothering to pause for her body to open to me, just forging ahead. She moaned and her hips pushed backwards.

"You want more?" I asked, adding a second finger with the same lack of gentleness.

"Yes," she answered on a slow moan.

"What do you say?"

"More please, Sir," she responded readily.

I pulled my fingers from her body and coated my cock liberally with lube before tucking the head of it at the clenching entrance of her ass. I gripped her hips hard, digging my fingers into the soft flesh of her curves as I surged forward. The first thrust opened her up. I felt her gasp even as it gave way to a needy little mewling sound. I pulled back just a little and thrust again. Her body opened for me a little more, the tight muscles letting me in a bit further. Another thrust, and another. Each time I sunk deeper into the heat of her body. The clench of her muscles around my cock, gripping it tight like a fist, made me groan.

"So fucking hot, Star," I told her. "Your ass is burning me. Are you burning?" I asked.

She nodded. "Please," she begged.

"You want more?" I asked.

"More please, Sir."

I sunk my cock deep until I bottomed out in her ass. Buried deep inside her, I slapped her ass with my open palm until the skin was red and angry. One side, then the other. Sometimes twice or more on a side before I switched. After her skin was flushed with blood at the surface, I gripped her hips again and fucked her hard and deep. My thumbs dug into the skin I'd just tenderized.

She whimpered. Her body trembling as her need ramped up.

I reached forward with one hand and wrapped a fist in her hair before hauling her to her knees by the strands. She screamed and her hands came over her head to grab my wrist. It wasn't to push me off though. It was to hold on. I watched over her shoulder as her breasts bounced with every thrust.

I kept my fist wrapped in her hair and my other hand went around her throat. My thumb brushed over the place where her pulse fluttered. "I'm going to be the reason you breathe," I whispered into her ear. "You'll ask for the pain only I can give you. And your body will be ready for me to use anytime I want. In the office. In the courthouse. Most importantly, in my bed."

She moaned, her body tightening even more around my cock. "Please, Sir," she begged.

"Beg me again," I demanded, my hand tightening around her throat a little. Not enough to cause any damage, but pressure that was just enough to give her pause.

"Please, Sir. Please, oh please."

It was music to my ears. Breathless, needy, lyrical words that I would never tire of hearing.

"I want you to come for me with my cock in your ass and your body completely in my control," I told her. "Let me feel you come apart right now. Mine. My Star." I let the demands fall from my lips. When I finished, I let my body push her over that edge. I fucked her hard, fast, and with a controlled ferocity that echoed in the air around us in the sounds of our bodies coming together with each thrust. She gasped in my arms, her nails digging into my forearm, where she still held tighter than the grip I had on her hair.

"Now, Star," I growled. "Come for me just like this and I'll paint your breasts in wax when we get home," I promised.

The flare of her eyes and the parting gasp on her lips told me she was remembering those drops of fire that had burned her so beautifully. Then she detonated in my arms. The orgasm that wracked her body was an stronger than any earthquake I'd felt before. Letting go, she exploded for me, she gave me the last bit of control over her. The ability to command her orgasms. I growled in her ear as my own release pulsed forth. I tightened my grip on her momentarily. Teasing her with that promise of more pain to come.

Afterwards, when I had cleaned us both up, she was back in my arms, her head resting on my chest as I ran my fingers through her hair and rubbed her back. The angry marks had finally calmed down enough that I could do so and give her pleasure from the pressure where she was sore. She hummed in response each time I hit a spot that made her feel good.

"Do you remember what I said to you just now?" I asked her.

She tensed a little in my arms, nodding slightly.

"And?" I prompted.

"What exactly are you asking for, Patrick?"

It was the use of my name that made me pause. But only for a moment. "I want you with me when we get back to Miami, Danica. I want you to be mine there too."

"For how long?" she asked.

"I can't say," I told her truthfully. "I don't want to promise something that doesn't happen. I don't want to tell you anything that I can't ensure." I paused, considering how I wanted to phrase what I would say. "What I can tell you is that I don't want to walk away without trying to see if we can work when we have other responsibilities and obligations."

"And if we can't?" she asked softly.

"We'll figure out next steps when we know what ones to take," I answered.

"You're asking for something that terrifies me," she said after long moments. Her words were so soft I almost didn't catch them.

"Why?" I asked.

"Because relying on someone else has never worked out for me."

I tightened my arms around her. "Have I ever done or said anything to make you think I would let you down?"

She grew still in my arms, barely breathing as I saw the wheels turning in her mind. Thinking. Searching for an answer. "No," she breathed.

"I have always been forthright with you, Dani. I've always said what I think and I don't hold it back. You can trust me to be the same way personally that I am at work." I paused and let that sink in before I added my requirement. "I have a condition for you though. In addition to moving in with me and submitting to me as my submissive."

"What's that?" she asked, cautious hesitation in her voice.

"If you're going to be my Star, I want you to shine in everything," I told her. "That means letting me add you onto my cases. You're not getting any extra special treatment. You're smart and you are the only one holding yourself back. Even before this, you know I felt that way. But I want you to change that. Stop holding yourself back when you have more than earned a place moving up the ladder."

I felt her take a deep breath. I felt the way she hesitated. And then, she gave me the answer I was looking for. "Okay."

I breathed deep, pleased and surprised. "You agree then?" I asked. "To all of it?"

"Yes, Sir."

~*~*~*~*~*~*~*~

Four hours later we stood at the dock and waited as our luggage was loaded onto the small seaplane that would take us back to Florida. Danica was saying her goodbye to Lance and I watched the man slip something into her hand before she turned away.

"What was that?" I asked.

She smiled and shook her head. "Lance is a bit full of himself."

"That he is," I agreed. Though she hadn't answered the question, which made me curious.

"If it becomes pertinent in the future, I'll let you know. But for now, it's just Lance thinking he's responsible for our new partnership," she told me after we were seated in the plane.

"Okay," I agreed.

She smiled and tucked her head against my shoulder. "There's a lot to do when we get back," she said as the plane moved away from the dock.

"There is. But you know what I think we should do first?"

She looked up at me and waited.

"Get you in my bed and in some straps that hold you still while I decorate your pretty breasts with wax."

Her breathing kicked up and I watched the way desire flooded her brown eyes, darkening them as her brain comprehended and her body responded. "Yes, Sir."

"The prettiest words from the prettiest lips," I said. I tipped her face up with a finger under her chin and leaned down to kiss her. "I promised you pain. I'll give you all that you need to find the pleasure you deserve, Star."

"Thank you, Sir," she sighed the words against my lips.

"That's my Star. Let's go home."

EPILOGUE

~DANICA~

It was three months and ten days after the broken condom when I knew for sure. I'd been able to put the thoughts and worries in the back of my mind for the most part with all the activity that had happened around me. But now that life was settling in private and in public, at work and in the home I now shared with Patrick, I realized I hadn't yet had my cycle. While that wasn't completely unusual, I was on a birth control shot, I also realized that I had missed my appointment for the next shot over a month before.

So now, looking at the little lines on the home pregnancy test that I'd bought on my way home, I knew. It appeared I had been right to worry all along. At least in regards to getting pregnant. I wasn't sure if it was from the broken condom or not. We were careful, of course, but that didn't mean there wasn't a possibility that another time had caused my condition. Once I went to a doctor, they would be able to tell me for sure the dates. That would help. Maybe.

I was still sitting at the kitchen table when Patrick came home. *Sir.* In the office, in public, he was Patrick. But here, in the privacy of our space, he was Sir. My Sir. And I was his Star.

I looked up as he walked through the door and watched as the curious expression became concern, then confusion, understanding, and finally a relaxed smile of acceptance.

"We'll take the steps we need to now that we know," he said. The words were achingly familiar. He spoke them often. Every time I had concerns or worries, he addressed them with the same calm acceptance and readiness to face the world with me, but to do it based on the knowledge we had and not the what ifs of the future.

"What steps do you think we should take?" I asked.

"First," he came close and lifted me into his arms, pressing a harsh kiss to my lips in greeting. When he lifted his head I was breathless. "What do you say?" he asked.

I shook my head. I needed some answers first.

He sighed, seeing my determination and carried me to our living room. He settled us on the couch and leaned back, still holding me tight. "Well, we'll need to consider a different location. An apartment in the middle of Miami's business district is not an ideal location to have a family. Plus, our spare room is a little non-child-friendly. While I want our baby to have a space, I'm not willing to give up our space either. So we need more room."

145   SECURING HIS STAR

I raised a hand and pressed a finger to his lips, pausing his words. "Okay," I said with a smile. "You're not mad?" I asked cautiously. After all, kids wasn't something we had ever discussed - at least, not since the condom had broken.

"I'm not mad, Star. If anything, I'm nervous. But that's because I don't know how I'll handle being a father. But I could never be mad at you. Not for this. And certainly not when something additional ties us together more than anything else in the world." He gazed down at me with those beautiful Irish eyes of his. "I love you."

I felt tears gathering in my eyes at his words. He hadn't said them before. Neither had I. Although given how quickly our relationship had changed and grown in the last few months, I couldn't say I was surprised either.

"I love you too," I responded easily, readily. Then I added the words he loved to hear, "More please, Sir."

"I'll give you more until I have nothing left to give," he promised.

Then he pressed his lips to mine once more and I let the worries about the future fade away for the moment. My Sir had me secure and safe in his arms, in his home, and in his life. And I had never felt like I belonged anywhere more than I did in that moment. I was home.

I was his Star.

~*~*~*~*~*~*~*~*~

THE END

~*~*~*~*~*~*~*~*~

LETTER FROM THE AUTHOR

Dear Reader,

Thank you for Reading and Welcome back to the Leather Persuasions Resort! I hope you enjoyed Patrick and Danica's story. If you did, please consider leaving a review on your favorite book site.

With 2022 firmly started, I'm keeping to the erotic side of things and if you missed my piece in the Flirty in Kansas City Anthology, don't worry. I'm going to be pulling it back out now and adding to the story. You'll see a solo release soon for Every Princess Deserves Fairy Lights & Booty Rubs.

Also coming up is a re-release of the Small Town Anthology paranormal novella, A Magickal Christmas Gift. That's coming this month.

Last, but definitely not least, I'll be returning to the Claimed series and finishing up the next book for that series.

I hope you'll stick around and explore some of the other books in the Leather Persuasions series, including my first one, Keeping His Kitten, if you haven't already done so.

Thank you,

~*Rexi*

SECURING HIS STAR

LEATHER PERSUASION RESORT SERIES - FIRST RELEASE

1. WORTH THE RISK - BY CRYSTAL LYNN & EVAN SHAW
2. BOUND TO YOU - BY CLAUDIA STEVENS
3. SECOND CHANCE PERSUASION - BY SIMONE EVANS
4. KEEPING HIS KITTEN - BY REXI LAKE
5. TIED TO THE BEAT - BY CATHERINE BOWMAN

LEATHER PERSUASION RESORT SERIES - SECOND RELEASE

6. CRAVE - BY CRYSTAL LYNN
7. YOURS TO TAME - BY CLAUDIA STEVENS
8. **
9. VOW - BY CATHERINE BOWMAN
10. SECURING HIS STAR - BY REXI LAKE
11. **
12. PETALS & STEEL - GREER RYLIE

LEATHER PERSUASION SERIES - EROTIC READERS BOOK CLUB FACEBOOK GROUP:
https://www.facebook.com/groups/2540934289471408/

WEBSITE:
https://authorcrystalstcla.wixsite.com/inspireme/leather-persuasion-series

About the Author

Rexi Lake is a dreamer. She lives in a world full of characters and their stories. And when she gets the time, she shares those stories with others. Rexi has always believed that the world deserves more happily ever afters, so she brings them into the world the best way she knows how: through her words. She lives in Western Pennsylvania with her socially active daughter. When she's not writing, she's busy with living and enjoying life and whatever comes her way.

You can find Rexi on a variety of social media sites, as well as her website. She does her best to attend 2-4 author events each year. Follow her for more information on upcoming releases and appearances.

OTHER NOVELS BY REXI LAKE

Just Say Yes World (Reading Order)

Claimed by Christmas (Claimed #1)

Claimed in Cuffs (Claimed #2)

Claimed in Chains (Claimed #3)

Claimed by the Chef: Turn Up the Heat (Claimed #4)

The World of the Imagi (Reading Order)

For the Love of Coffee (Fated Mates #1)

For the Love of Chocolate (Fated Mates #2)

Mistletoe Magic (Fated Mates #2.5)

Eric's Eternity (Eternal Steel #0.5)

A Magickal Christmas Gift (Fated Mates #2.7/True Heart #0.5)

Re-release

Fairyfales

Wicked for Him #1

Being Her Beast #2

Spirit Hollow

Sips and Spells and Wedding Bells

Standalones

Keeping His Kitten (Leather Persuasion Multi-Author Series)

Securing His Star (Leather Persuasion Multi-Author Series)

The Lady of the Lake (Loch Gaoil Multi-Author Series)

Sweet Cider Sin (Bad Apples Multi-Author Series)

His Guiding Light (Forever Safe Christmas II)

His Christmas Rose (Forever Safe: The Twelve Days of Christmas)

The Hitman's Fall *Re-release*

Anthologies

Eternal Steel Beginnings (Hearts of Steel Charity Anthology) *Original Version of Eric's Eternity*

The Hitman's Fall (Heart of an Alpha Charity Anthology) *Original Release*

A Magickal Christmas Gift (A Small Town Christmas Charity Anthology) *Original Release*

Every Princess Deserves Fairy Lights & Booty Rubs (Flirty in Kansas City Anthology) *Original Release*

Coming Soon

Stealing Her Heart (Fairyfales)

**Note: All Anthologies were released for a limited time. The stories in each are released as individual books once the limited time has passed. Re-released stories are noted only if they are identical to the anthology piece. If the story was significantly altered, it is noted under the anthologies as an "Original Version" and not listed as a "Re-release."

TURN THE PAGE FOR THE FIRST CHAPTER OF:

KEEPING HIS KITTEN

LEATHER PERSUASION 4

BY REXI LAKE

CHAPTER ONE

KELLI

I looked at the envelope Kristin had thrust into my hands as she gave me one last hug before jumping into the elegant limo. She was off on her next adventure, a month long honeymoon cruise, and I was left behind.

Okay, I wasn't actually left behind. In fact, I was anything but left behind.

My sister, *my twin,* had taken it upon herself to give me something of my own just as she was embarking on her own: an all expenses paid, two week long, Carribean vacation.

I stared out the tiny window of the little plane as it sped across the sky from Miami to the Virgin Island of St. John. The little seaplane I'd boarded was the smallest I'd ever been in and while the ride itself was smooth, I could imagine a strong wind easily knocking the plane into the water below us.

Of course, the water was where I felt safest. The cool waves that ebbed and flowed with a rhythm that could rock a person to sleep were my haven. In Jubilee Harbor, my Connecticut home, I was the half owner of a wildlife rescue and release program. While Kristin handled the land animals and all things furry, I took care of the aquatic wildlife. The turtles and dolphins, a variety of fish and small creatures lived in the tanks and enclosures I'd carefully constructed to replicate their natural habitats. Many were successfully released back into their watery homes, but a few wouldn't survive the wild waves.

I'd left them behind for these few weeks. I wasn't worried about the program. We had plenty of solid employees who were capable of running the place in our absence. But thinking about work helped keep me from fidgeting in my seat as the plane started to descend to the waters below and the dock of the exclusive resort where I was about to be completely out of my element.

When I'd boarded the seaplane, there were two couples already waiting for takeoff. While I'd sat slightly away from them, not wanting to encourage conversation with strangers, their words and giggles had been hard to ignore. I wasn't going to a resort that catered to rest and relaxation. Kristin had pushed me into the heart of my deepest secrets. A kink resort. She'd booked me a two week getaway at a place that was filled with fantasies and kinky fun for its guests. I had no idea what that meant, what I would see or do, what to even expect. So I gripped the invitation tightly and stared out the window some more as the plane dipped lower in the sky before finally touching down on the calm surface of the warm sea waters.

~*~*~*~*~*~*~*~

Leather Persuasion Resort was exactly what I expected a resort to look like. Except for the twelve foot wall that surrounded the place. Taking my time to look around me, I let the others enter the large building at the end of the dock first. I glanced down the beach and immediately averted my gaze as I caught sight of a couple locked in an embrace that I probably could have handled if they'd been clothed.

Looking down the other way, I saw a much tamer view. Some blankets were spread out along the beach and while there was definitely *more* happening than just relaxing in the sunshine, at least the bodies were clothed in swimsuits and the like. I wasn't a voyeur though, so my gaze returned to the building before me and I stepped forward, dragging my slightly battered, rolling suitcase behind me.

"Welcome!"

I smiled politely, a little taken aback by the British sounding gentleman that suddenly appeared before me. He was perfectly dressed in a deep midnight blue blazer over a crisp white polo. Even his hair, a sun-kissed blond, was expertly styled and the breeze that flowed through the open doorway of the main building stopped just short of him, not daring to muss his perfect coiffure.

"Hello," I murmured.

"My dear, you must be Kelli. I'm Lance, your architect of adventure while you are here. Whatever you might desire, simply whisper it my way and your wish will be granted. Like a fairy godmother, but much better dressed and without that silly wand. My, you are simply divine, aren't you?"

The question didn't seem to need an answer as his gaze traversed my form not just once, but enough times to almost make me feel like a piece of meat. Almost.

"You know," he placed a single finger on the side of his cheek, "I bet you would look marvelous with some strawberry blonde highlights and a bright red sundress." He waved his hand in a fluttering motion. "Oh. I can just see it now. We do have a spa nearby that does fabulous work. If you're interested." He arched a brow at me.

"Uh, maybe after I get settled in?" I made sure to end my thought with a question. I was more than ready to find a room and then perhaps a stroll along the beach. Or a swim. A swim sounded really great, especially after spending way too much time in the air.

"Of course, sweetie. Let's get you settled and then I can give you the grand tour and we can figure out what you want to do while you're here." He swung around and snapped his fingers. A man I hadn't even noticed appeared and took possession of my suitcases. He attempted to take my personal bag as well, but that wasn't leaving my side.

"No, I'll keep this with me," I told him.

He paused, then nodded. He was a large man, muscled and big in that bulky, Hulk-like way that should have been intimidating but really wasn't when the person in question was wearing a dog mask over his face, a collar tight around his neck, and an outfit that left nothing to the imagination. The tight black shorts were barely bigger than a Speedo. I averted my eyes, looking back toward my self-appointed *adventure architect*.

"Don't worry about him, sweetie," Lance told me. "His master sent him over for a punishment. He's not allowed to speak until his shift is over. You'll find that happens with some of our staff members. Punishments during work, that is. Everyone here lives the Lifestyle as well as working in it."

"The Lifestyle?" I asked. I'd heard about such things - people living in a power exchange dynamic - but I'd never seen it before. And reading it in those books I kept hidden in my nightstand probably didn't count for much either. I had no idea how much of what I'd read was fiction and how much was fact. But the only person who I'd ever revealed my interest to had taken that knowledge and tossed me to the wolves.

Okay, maybe it wasn't the wolves. She'd definitely placed me outside my comfort zone but it was in a place where I could dive and swim to my heart's content. So I couldn't be too upset with her.

Lance paused and reached over the registration counter. He grabbed a set of keys before he turned back around to me. He handed one key to the man who had my bags. "She's in cabin 4." I watched as the silent giant disappeared with my stuff. "Cabin 4 is on the Cove side of the resort," Lance said, pulling my attention back around. "Now, sweetie, let's give you a bit of a tour and then we'll see what you want to set up while you're staying with us. There's some rather phenomenal things that we have available. Everything from seminars to demos and of course, there's the playrooms as well."

"Playrooms?" Damn my sister. She'd given me no time to research this place. I'd gotten a handful of information from the things I'd overheard on the plane, but apparently there was a whole lot more to this resort than a little extra privacy and kink.

"Kelli, sweetie, I know this was booked for you by your sister, but she assured me that you had knowledge of the Lifestyle." Lance looked at me, the slightest crease in his brow and slight turn downward of his lips the only change that gave away his concern.

"She may have exaggerated," I said. "I've read a few things and I'm intrigued by some of it, but that's about as much as I know." I shrugged. I was sure Kristin hadn't omitted anything on purpose. In fact, she was a fairly straight-forward type of person. But she wasn't interested in anything kinky, so how would she know the extent? I certainly didn't.

"Oh." That single word was drawn out on a long breath. Then he straightened and grinned with a level of glee that put me in mind of my mother when Kristin had said she was getting married. That glint of extreme happiness was terrifying.

I took the slightest step backward. "Maybe we could do a tour a little later?" I asked, wondering if it was too late to turn around and reboard the plane. "I'd really like to relax a little and maybe just enjoy the beach for today."

"Absolutely!" Lance agreed, a little too readily. "Come with me. Let's get you settled and I'll point out the places you can get some food." He looped my arm around his and guided me back the way we'd come. "There's three ways to get meals here. You can dine in the restaurant in this building." He pointed to a side entrance that I'd overlooked in my initial perusal. "You can order room service from your cabin. Or you can go to one of the local places outside the resort. We do have a shuttle that runs into the towns for the usual tourist stuff - shopping, spas, cousine, etcetera."

"I've heard there's some great areas to snorkel and dive around the island," I said. We were walking down a winding path toward a small set of cabins. I glanced toward the waves that glided gently against the sand. There was just the slightest breeze that brought with it the scent of the sea. Salty and fresh, and with that come hither whisper that called to me.

"Oh, yes. There's a reef right here that's quite amazing." He stopped in front of a small cabin. The door had the number '4' stenciled onto it in a large, bold font. "In fact, one of the local bars is a very popular spot for scuba divers. It's just in the next bay, but the little thing is only accessible from the water. I'll send over a map and some general information about the reefs and the hidden bays. Gear is available to rent at the main desk, or if you want, I can send someone over with what you'll need now."

"No need," I shook my head and smiled as I spoke. "I brought my own. But the map and info would be great." I could certainly use that. "Is there internet?" I asked.

"In limited supply, yes. We don't allow recordings in any of the general play areas, but inside your cabin and on the beach over here, you are welcome to take photos and use the internet." Lance twisted the knob and pushed open the door. He bowed, a courtly gesture that seemed out of place in the midst of a kinky beach paradise, but he did it with a style all his own.

"I have no intention of recording anyone else," I assured him as I stepped past into the spacious living area.

"I'm sure Michael placed your bags just inside the bedroom," Lance said as he stepped beside me. He pointed to a nearby door that was closed. "The bathroom is through the bedroom, and the kitchen is moderately stocked with a few necessities. Like coffee." He winked and gestured to the back door. "You can walk right out the back onto a private deck. The fence that surrounds it is high enough to allow for privacy for any *activities* you might choose to enjoy. The beach on this side is traditional. Clothing required. When you are ready for that tour, call my extension - three-six-nine - and I'll be happy to help you find what you're looking for."

"I'm only looking for a few weeks to relax," I said hastily. Really. I wasn't so sure about Kristin's gift. Now that I was here, I was definitely feeling those nerves getting all sorts of twisted up in my stomach. Diving first. Maybe that would help me find the courage to cross the resort to take part in the other activities.

He nodded, but I could see the wheels in his head spinning just enough as he contemplated me with that slight smirk. His eyes seemed to acknowledge me in a way that I couldn't quite grasp the meaning of. Then he blinked and the look was gone, replaced by the smooth features and bright smile that had greeted me at the beginning.

"You settle in and I'll send that info right away, sweetie. It's our goal, here at Leather Persuasions, to ensure that every guest enjoys their time to the fullest. If there is anything else you need while you're here, you have only to ask. We are here to serve."

I smiled my thanks as he again gave me a courtly bow and left me alone in the cabin.

I went into the bedroom first, ready to grab my gear and get ready. But the moment my eyes caught sight of the beautiful king-sized bed with the softest looking pillows and crisp white comforter, I remembered just how tired I was from the past forty-eight hours. Toeing off my shoes, I crawled up onto the bed and relaxed into the most comfortable bed I'd ever been in. A short nap wouldn't hurt.

I drifted off to sleep as the soft sound of waves lapping at the shoreline filtered through the quiet.

Made in the USA
Middletown, DE
19 March 2022

62805612R00096